# 36 Hours

## Book One

## The Blackout Series

A novel by

Bobby Akart

**Copyright Information**

Thank you for purchasing
36 Hours by Bobby Akart

For free advance reading copies, updates on new releases,
special offers, and bonus content,
Sign Up at BobbyAkart.com:

BobbyAkart.com

# Other Works by Bestselling Author Bobby Akart

## The Pandemic Series

*Beginnings*

*The Innocents*

*Level 6*

*Quietus*

## The Blackout Series

*36 Hours*

*Zero Hour*

*Turning Point*

*Shiloh Ranch*

*Hornet's Nest*

*Devil's Homecoming*

## The Boston Brahmin Series

*The Loyal Nine*

*Cyber Attack*

*Martial Law*

*False Flag*

*The Mechanics*

*Choose Freedom!*

*Seeds of Liberty (Companion Guide)*

## The Prepping for Tomorrow Series

*Cyber Warfare*

*EMP: Electromagnetic Pulse*

*Economic Collapse*

# DEDICATIONS

To the love of my life, thank you for making the sacrifices necessary
so I may pursue this dream.

To the *Princesses of the Palace*, my little marauders in training, you have
no idea how much happiness you bring to your mommy and me.

To my fellow preppers—never be ashamed of adopting
a preparedness lifestyle.

# ACKNOWLEDGEMENTS

Writing a book that is both informative and entertaining requires a tremendous team effort. Writing is the easy part. For their efforts in making The Blackout Series a reality, I would like to thank Hristo Argirov Kovatliev for his incredible cover art, Pauline Nolet and Sabrina Jean for making my important work reader-friendly, Stef Mcdaid for making this manuscript decipherable on so many formats, and The Team—whose advice, friendship and attention to detail is priceless.

The Blackout Series could not have been written without the tireless counsel and direction from those individuals who shall remain nameless at the Space Weather Prediction Center in Boulder, Colorado and at the Atacama Large Millimeter Array (ALMA) in Chile. Thank you for providing me a portal into your observations and data.

Lastly, a huge thank you to Dr. Tamitha Skov, a friend and social media icon, who is a research scientist at The Aerospace Corporation in Southern California. With her PHD in Geophysics and Space Plasma Physics, she has become a vital resource for amateur astronomers and aurora watchers around the world. Without her insight, The Blackout Series could not have been written. Visit her website at http://www.SpaceWeatherWoman.com.

Thank you!

# ABOUT THE AUTHOR

## Bobby Akart

Bestselling author Bobby Akart has been ranked by Amazon worldwide as the #3 Bestselling Religion & Spirituality Author, the #5 Bestselling Science Fiction Author, and the #7 Bestselling Historical Author. He is the author of sixteen international bestsellers, in thirty-nine different fiction and nonfiction genres, including his latest project, The Pandemic Series, the critically acclaimed Boston Brahmin series, the bestselling Blackout series, and his highly cited nonfiction Prepping for Tomorrow series.

Bobby has provided his readers a diverse range of topics that are both informative and entertaining. His attention to detail and impeccable research has allowed him to capture the imaginations of his readers through his fictional works, and bring them valuable knowledge through his nonfiction books.

**SIGN UP FOR EMAIL UPDATES** and receive free advance reading copies, updates on new releases, special offers, and bonus content. You can contact Bobby directly by email (BobbyAkart@gmail.com) or through his website:

## www.BobbyAkart.com

# ABOUT THE BLACKOUT SERIES

*WHAT WOULD YOU DO*
if a voice was screaming in your head – *GET READY* . . .
for a catastrophic event of epic proportions . . .
with no idea where to start . . .
or how, or when?

*This is a true story, it just hasn't happened yet.*

A new dystopian, post-apocalyptic fiction series from sixteen-time international best selling author Bobby Akart (The Pandemic Series, The Blackout Series, The Boston Brahmin series, and the Prepping for Tomorrow series).

The characters depicted in The Blackout Series are fictional. The events, however, are based upon fact.

This is not the story of preppers with stockpiles of food, weapons, and a hidden bunker. This is the story of Colton Ryman, his stay-at-home wife, Madison, and their teenage daughter, Alex. In 36 Hours, the Ryman family and the rest of the world will be thrust into the darkness of a post-apocalyptic world.

A catastrophic solar flare, an EMP—a threat from above to America's soft underbelly below—is hurtling toward our planet.

The Rymans have never heard of preppers and have no concept of what prepping entails. But they're learning, while they run out of time. Their faith will be tested, their freedom will be threatened, but their family will survive.

An EMP, naturally generated from our sun in the form of a solar flare, has happened before, and it will happen again, in only 36 Hours.

This is a story about how our sun, the planet's source of life, can also devastate our modern world. It's a story about panic, chaos, and the final straws that shattered an already thin veneer of civility. It is a warning to us all ...

*never underestimate the depravity of man.*

What would you do when the clock strikes zero?
Midnight is forever.

**Note**: This book does not contain strong language. It is intended to entertain and inform audiences of all ages, including teen and young adults. Although some scenes depict the realistic threat our nation faces from a devastating solar flare, and the societal collapse which will result in the aftermath, it does not contain graphic scenes typical of other books in the post-apocalyptic genre.

# EPIGRAPH

Here comes the sun. Here comes the sun, and I say, it's all right.
~ the quiet Beatle
*****

Civilization is hideously fragile.
There's not much between us & the horrors underneath, just about a
coat of varnish.
~ CP Snow
*****

TEOTWAWKI—The End of The World As We Know It
It is not, however, the end of the world.
*****

By failing to prepare, you are preparing to fail.
~ Benjamin Franklin
*****

I would rather be wrong and alive, than oblivious and dead.
~ Bobby Akart
*****

Because you never know when the day before
is the day before.
Prepare for tomorrow!

# Prologue

**10:00 p.m., September 8, Thursday**
**MISSION CONTROL CENTER**
**Houston, Texas**

From the ground, space looks like a pristine void—fascinating, miraculous, serene. But the Earth's orbit is actually a very crowded place inhabited by twenty-four hundred satellites and many thousands of pieces of space junk.

The altitude above the planet containing the vast majority of this debris, and some of mankind's most used spacecraft, is between one hundred miles and twelve hundred miles above the Earth's surface. This is known as the low Earth orbit, and it's home to the International Space Station.

In 2009, the first accidental collision between two low Earth orbiting satellites occurred when the two-thousand-pound Russian-made Kosmos-2251 collided with the slightly smaller U.S.-built Iridium-33 communications satellite launched on behalf of the satellite telephone provider.

As was customary, after the Kosmos-2251 had been deactivated, it was left in Earth's orbit as space debris. On February tenth of that year, the Iridium-33 sped through its orbit five hundred miles above Earth at approximately twenty-six thousand miles per hour.

NASA estimated the collision, seen by amateur astronomers from Japan to Europe, created over a thousand pieces of debris. Russian and Chinese scientists immediately warned all relevant space agencies worldwide that the debris would pose a threat to satellites and the International Space Station.

NASA assembled its team and, in coordination with the ISS crew, deftly executed a collision-avoidance maneuver to avoid a large piece of the orbital debris caused by the space pileup. Fortunately, the Christopher C. Kraft Jr. Mission Control Center, or MCC, in Houston was fully operational at the time. Tracking data on the space debris was readily available, and predictions were performed, which led to a fairly accurate probability for a mid-space collision.

The 2009 near-miss was not the only time NASA orchestrated collision-avoidance maneuvers with the ISS. On one occasion, the threat of a crash in orbit was so great that NASA ordered six members of the ISS crew to enter Russian Soyuz transport ships for a possible evacuation.

As a result of these events, protocols and procedures were established. Space debris was monitored and warnings were shared, all in cooperation with the major space agencies around the world—except one.

China had lost control of its Tiangong-1 space station. Their Manned Space Engineering Office had not made an announcement of the mission failure for fear the Beijing government's alternate purpose—carrying a nuclear payload, would be discovered. The Chinese military developed an EMP warhead capable of being launched from space. It was the first of its kind and was known within the People's Liberation Army as *The Great Equalizer*. Now, the crowning achievement in Chinese military history was hurtling out of control in low Earth orbit.

Weighing nearly twenty thousand pounds and soaring around

Earth at a speed of seventeen thousand miles per hour, the Tiangong-1 became an immediate danger to every spacecraft in its path. The intense geomagnetic storm engulfing Earth impacted orbiting satellites and the modular space stations first. NASA's ability to track unresponsive space debris was hampered. They had to rely upon sight visuals and data transmitted from the ISS.

ISS: "We copy, Houston. We are feeling the effects of the solar wind at this point. I have to say the aurora is stunning. The dancing lights must be putting on quite a spectacular show down there. I can tell you I've never seen anything like it."

MCC: "Roger that, Commander. I don't want to lead you astray, but data analysis and monitoring on our end is fragmentary at best. This G5 storm is unprecedented. We're not your eyes and ears on the ground that you're accustomed to."

ISS: "Copy, Houston. Our Navigation and Controls Systems appear to be fully operational. All near-object warning systems appear to be functioning and quiet at this time. The systems engineer is monitoring the Data Display System. The remainder of the crew is disbursed to provide visuals."

MCC: "Roger, Commander. As conditions change, will advise. Still no official word from the Chinese."

ISS: "Copy, Houston. My Russian counterpart had a few choice words for his neighbor to the south that I couldn't repeat if I tried. Suffice it to say they sounded *harsh*."

MCC: "Roger. Those sentiments have been expressed throughout the MCC. Stand by, Commander."


**11:00 p.m., September 8**
**INTERNATIONAL SPACE STATION**
**254 Miles Above Earth**


If you think of the Sun as a giant bubble of boiling water, then the solar wind would be the wisps of steam that float away from the surface. The Sun is always simmering, sending off clouds, or tendrils, of high-energy puffs of particles called coronal mass ejections. Before these high-energy winds strike Earth at roughly nine hundred miles per hour, they smash into Earth-orbiting satellites first.

Although satellites have built-in protections against normal levels of solar wind, intense bursts like the ones being experienced on this night can overwhelm these protections and destroy onboard electronic systems.

These solar wind particles increased the aurora phenomena in Earth's atmosphere. The crew of the ISS was busy monitoring the data available to them, but they couldn't resist the opportunity to snap a few pictures to be posted later.

As the solar wind hit Earth's magnetic field, it dissipated and transferred its energy to the ions in the atmosphere. This resulted in the magnificent view enjoyed by the ISS team. It also resulted in the ions being rerouted into the upper layers of the ionosphere—disrupting the operations of the Global Positioning System.

While the crew of the four-hundred-and-fifty-ton ISS was distracted by the beauty of the aurora, their onboard navigation system adjusted their orbit based upon false readings from the GPS. The new altitude was consistent with another space station no longer within the control of man nor computer—the Tiandong-1.

The collision between the two space stations resembled an eighteen-wheel gasoline tanker running over a parked Volkswagen at eighty miles an hour—the VW would get the worst of the impact, but both would suffer serious damage. In this accident, the crash was magnified by the payload of the Tiandong-1.

The nuclear explosion, and the incredible inferno produced by it, fused the two spacecraft into an asteroid-sized hunk of steel. Earth's weakened atmosphere as a result of the geomagnetic storm opened a portal for the electromagnetic radiation and the remains of the two space stations.

The timing of the conflagration couldn't have been worse.

## 11:03 p.m., September 8
## The Pacific Ocean

Returning a spacecraft to Earth is tricky business primarily because of the intense heat produced. A miscalculation can have a profound impact on the debris. If the re-entry is uncontrolled, as space debris enters Earth's atmosphere, it explodes into molten metal. The size and speed depends on the conditions in the atmosphere at the time.

Satellites, and their rocket boosters, do fall from space, re-entering the atmosphere. Earth's gravity field, atmospheric drag, solar conditions, and even ocean tides caused by the gravitational attraction of the moon all impact the drop from orbit and the resulting descent.

Most times, the satellites break up into thousands of pieces and land harmlessly in one of the planet's vast oceans. But in times of intense geomagnetic storms, Earth's magnetosphere is weakened, which in turn allows solar wind and particles to slam into the planet.

Likewise, space debris, after it has become a heavier mass of metal, can travel at a greater velocity towards Earth's surface. A major impact event releases the energy of several nuclear weapons detonating simultaneously. For example, a three-mile wide asteroid could result in an extinction-level event.

After the collision, the resulting forty-four thousand metric tonnes of molten metal was two hundred feet wide as it screamed through the sky at nearly forty thousand miles per hour. Like most satellite remnants from the past, the remains of the ISS and Tiangong soared toward one of the world's vast oceans. It would make impact halfway between Hawaii and the coast of Baja, California.

Later, after many, many years, it was estimated that the total kinetic energy at the time of impact was equivalent to two thousand kilotons of TNT, over one hundred times more energy than was released from the atomic bomb detonated at Hiroshima. Ordinarily, the bulk of the object's energy would be absorbed by the atmosphere.

Not on this day, at this time. It was Zero Hour.

# Thirty-Six Hours Earlier

# Chapter 1

**36 Hours**
**11:00 a.m., September 7, Wednesday**
**ALMA**
**Atacama, Chile**

Dr. Andrea Stanford wheeled the vintage Toyota Land Cruiser up the winding dirt road to the summit of the mountain desert. The Atacama Desert is considered one of the driest places on Earth. Surrounded by two mountain ranges of the Andes and just south of the Chile-Bolivia border, it is made up of salt basins and lava flows that are over twenty million years old. Large volcanoes dominate the landscape, including Láscar, the most active in Chile.

Because of its otherworldly appearance and inhospitable climate, the Atacama Desert was useless except to movie producers filming exoplanet-like scenes, and NASA, who duplicated tests used by the Viking I and Viking II Mars landers to detect life. Oddly, during their practice runs, they were unable to detect life in the Atacama Desert soil.

However, Atacama's uniqueness created the ideal conditions to search for life elsewhere—the universe. Its dryness, high altitude, nearly nonexistent cloud cover, and lack of light pollution or radio interference made the peak of the Atacama Desert one of the best places in the world to conduct astronomical observations.

At an altitude of over sixteen thousand feet, Atacama, Chile, was the home of the largest telescope on the planet—the Atacama Large Millimeter Array, or ALMA.

The gravel spun under her tires as she rounded the final bend to the summit. The rear end of the lightweight vehicle side slipped until Dr. Stanford corrected her course. She could feel the adrenaline pumping through her body and slowed to avoid crashing to the gulch below.

Despite being involved in the design and construction of ALMA during its developmental stage, she continued to be awestruck as the massive observatory complex came into view.

Sixty-six dish antennas measuring forty feet across dotted the arid landscape. A unique portable system was designed that consisted of enormous transporters resembling a sixteen-wheel moon rover. Resting on their chassis were the antennas—mobile and ready for orders. Three of the vehicles were in motion as they gently hauled around the massive antennas to form arrays dictated by the ALMA observatory scientists in the control room. The more compact the arrays, the better the scientists could observe large, dimmer objects. The widespread formation allowed the scientists to focus on the finer details of a particular celestial body.

Dr. Stanford exited her truck and was greeted by a gust of cool, dry wind to which she had become accustomed. Born and raised in Las Vegas, a *breezy day*, as described by the local television meteorologist, which typically consisted of sixty-mile-per-hour winds, would be at near-hurricane strength to a resident of Florida, sending them scurrying to the local Home Depot for plywood and batteries. It was a chilly thirty-four degrees as she started a workday that would change her life forever.

"Good morning, Dr. Stanford," greeted her longtime assistant, Jose Cortez, one of the program managers on the Joint Alma Observatory—JAO—Team.

"Good morning, Jose," she replied with a smile. "I see the gentle giants are on the move already," she added, referring to the antenna transporters.

"Yes, ma'am, per your instructions. The systems astronomers have run the calculations, and we are in position as our target region comes into view."

She handed Jose her briefcase and peeled off her jacket, draping it over his outstretched arm. "Coffee, my friend, and make it so black that Juan Valdez would be proud." She laughed.

"You've got it, boss, and, by the way, NASA's called already."

"Of course they have."

Dr. Stanford was born enjoying the wonders of the universe. As a child, she studied astronomy and invested the money she made babysitting into amateur telescopes. While many of the kids in her astronomy club focused on faraway galaxies, Dr. Stanford became fascinated with the celestial body most familiar to us all—the sun. By the time she turned twenty-one and graduated near the top of her class at UNLV, she had seen it rise and fall nearly seventy-five hundred times.

While studying astronomy at the Harvard-Smithsonian Center for Astrophysics in Cambridge, Massachusetts, she became convinced there was still a lot that science didn't know about the star at the center of our solar system. Dr. Stanford believed the study of the sun was the one area of astronomy that had relevance to our daily life. Our sun gave us life, but it was also the most potentially dangerous threat to humanity.

The sun is as unpredictable as it is predictable. It remains in a relatively fixed position while its temperatures stay fairly constant. Yet, occasionally, it erupts with an intense, high-energy blast of radiation released into space. As sunspots form on the surface, stored energy in the magnetic fields above the sunspots is suddenly released. In a matter of moments, they heat up to many millions of degrees and produce a solar flare.

This fascinated Dr. Stanford, and she devoted her career to the study of other stars similar to our sun. Her career enabled her to define our sun's activities better by learning, indirectly, from examples set by celestial bodies in other solar systems.

"Good morning, all," she announced as she entered the sophisticated control room of ALMA. She received a variety of responses from the JAO Team, but they were subdued. Everyone was focused on their respective consoles, studying data and waiting for the guest of honor to make its appearance.

"Doc, our target should be rotating into view shortly," said Deb Daniels, one of the senior astronomers who had remained on deck all night, waiting for this moment. "I'll bring it up on the big screens."

Four seventy-inch computer screens mounted on the wall of the control room came to life. Each monitor had a different view of the sun provided by their antennae and the GOES Satellite system monitored by NASA.

GOES was an acronym for Geostationary Operational Environmental Satellite system. The National Weather Service used the GOES system for its weather monitoring and forecasting operations. Scientific researchers, like the team at ALMA, used the data to study space weather, especially the sun's activity.

A large monitor revealed a view of Earth that identified major storm systems around the globe, together with temperatures at the various layers of Earth's atmosphere. Another display revealed data related to the magnetosphere, the region surrounding Earth created by Earth's north and south poles. The magnetosphere buffers Earth from the devastating effects of solar wind. Without the magnetosphere, the surface of Earth would look like Mars.

The third monitor displayed a series of solar wind dials, measuring data like density, speed, magnitude, and direction. These conditions were critical to space weather prediction.

Finally, the monitor drawing the most attention of the scientists at ALMA that day provided the latest images from SOHO—the Solar and Heliospheric Observatory. These solar snapshots revealed activity on the sun's surface such as coronal holes, low-density regions of the sun's atmosphere that were the source of high-speed winds of solar particles that streamed off the sun into space. As a coronal hole released the sun's magnetic fields, soaring up and away from the surface, they created the conditions necessary for a solar flare.

Dr. Stanford turned her attention to Jose, who had returned with her coffee. She took a sip and allowed the rush of steaming caffeine to hit her body. She doubted the jolt was needed, as excitement-fueled anxiety would be readily available.

"Thank you, Jose," said Dr. Stanford, who then asked Daniels, "Deb, do we have a designation yet?"

"The next numbered active region will be 3222," replied Daniels.

Dr. Stanford took another sip of coffee. She muttered under her breath, "Show yourself, AR3222."

The room remained quiet as the sun slowly rotated on the screen. Twenty-four hours prior, a coronal hole developed and released a series of non-earth directed X-flares. Solar flares were rated as class B, C, N, or X, with X-class being the most powerful.

This active region released an X1.8-class solar flare as its final hurrah yesterday. The bright flash of light observed on the SOHO monitors was the largest of the year so far. But it didn't approach the more massive X20 flares of April 2001 and August 1989. Twenty times the size of yesterday's eruption, those flares caused massive power outages in the northern United States and Canada.

Yesterday, the coronal hole caught the attention of the JAO Team because it was expanding upon the sun's surface as it rotated out of view. Dr. Stanford knew if the trend continued, today could be a potentially historic solar event.

In the same hemisphere of the sun as yesterday's eruption, a sunspot region appeared on the disk that followed the same trajectory as the previous AR. The monitors began to reveal more. At first, two coronal holes appeared—clustered together. The sun continued to rotate.

"Whoa," Jose leaned in and whispered into Dr. Stanford's ear.

"My God," she said aloud. Dr. Stanford watched in amazement as the largest coronal hole ever recorded rotated into view, followed by two smaller voids. The entire active region consumed the northern hemisphere of the sun.

AR3222 was now on full display.

# CHAPTER 2

**36 Hours**
**11:00 a.m., September 7**
**Dallas Cowboys—AT&T Stadium**
**Arlington, Texas**

"Nice throw. Nice throw!" yelled Jerry Jones, owner of the Dallas Cowboys, as he applauded a throw by his rookie quarterback from Mississippi State which hit his all-pro receiver right in the numbers. Jones turned to his entourage and continued. "Did you see that kid hit Dez on the go route? He has to make that throw perfectly, hitting his target in stride. That's NFL precision from a fourth-round pick!"

Colton Ryman smiled and nodded as if he knew what the owner of the most lucrative sports franchise in history was talking about. Colton enjoyed watching football, but he wasn't into the nuances of the game, and clearly had no clue what a *go route* was.

Colton's passion was music. It was in his blood. His ancestor, Captain Thomas Ryman, built the Union Gospel Tabernacle in Nashville in the late eighteen hundreds, but it wasn't until his death in 1904 that the building became known as Ryman Auditorium.

In 1925, an insurance company installed a radio station in the auditorium that had been designed to replace the traditional revival tent used by his friend Reverend Sam Jones. WSM, which stood for *We Shield Millions*—the company's motto—started a tradition of country music in Nashville beginning with the Grand Ole Opry and continuing with the concerts of the biggest stars of today. The rest was history.

Jones continued with the tour of AT&T Stadium, home of the Dallas Cowboys since 2008. "Last year, we enjoyed playing at

Wembley Stadium in London, but it was a logistical nightmare for team operations. On a personal basis, and speaking for the Dallas Cowboys, we would very much like a team in London. It has cachet. It has an air about it of international competition. It would be good for the league."

*And good for your wallet, I suspect.* Colton might not understand the finer points of football, but he understood the intricacies of the entertainment business. Jerry Jones was a master of entertainment, and the NFL was his playing field. Colton was honored to be in the *game*.

At thirty-nine, Colton had reached the top echelons of the entertainment and media business. Born in Austin, Texas, and with the Ryman blood flowing through his veins, he longed for a country music career. Music became his life, but he quickly learned that opportunities for guitar-pickin' cowboys were slim and talent was abundant.

Colton discovered he had a genetic disposition toward business. When the Ryman family migrated from Chattanooga, Tennessee to the hill country of Central Texas along with Davy Crockett in 1835, they became known as traders and merchants. From Fort Worth to Austin, the Ryman name became synonymous with cattle and oil. He learned the art of business and negotiation from his daddy, who learned from his daddy before him.

The summer before he started college at SMU in Dallas, he hung out around the music venues of the Dallas metroplex. From the White Elephant Saloon and Billy Bob's in Fort Worth to Adair's in Dallas, Colton enjoyed the sights and sounds of country music.

The day he announced his decision to forego his education at SMU for the entertainment and media management curriculum at UCLA, his momma cried. She wasn't ready to lose her only son to the real world yet. At SMU, she could have kept an eye on Colton and protected him. But his daddy was proud of his decision. Colton was a born negotiator and was pursuing his passion, just like the Rymans before him.

Jones took Colton's client by the arm and led him onto the field as the practice session began to break up. Kenny Chesney had already signed as the lead performer for the upcoming Super Bowl hosted by Dallas, and the rest of the talent was being lined up. His client, Eric Church, was working his way up the Billboard charts as one of the top country artists in the nation. Securing a position in the Super Bowl halftime show would be a huge boost for his popularity and a monumental leap for Colton's career.

As managing partner of United Talent's Nashville office, he was already one of the most respected figures in the business. But after the most watched television program in history featured two decades of rap and rock performances, this was a rare opportunity for him to insert his country stock into the biggest spectacle in television entertainment—the Super Bowl.

"Whadya think, Colton?" asked Church. "You think we can pack this house?"

"Dang straight!" replied Colton.

"I think they wanna bring in Keith to do 'Raise 'Em Up' with me. How the heck am I gonna keep my feet on the ground for the next five months?"

"That's my job, buddy," replied Colton, trying to control his own emotional high. *Who's gonna keep my feet on the ground?*

Church approached Colton and spoke quietly. "What kinda numbers we talkin', Mr. Agent?"

"We'll go over that in the morning, hoss," replied Colton. "You've gotta gig tonight and I don't need you distracted. I have another meeting with the NFL folks tomorrow before you and I can talk."

Colton didn't have the heart to tell Church that his paycheck from the NFL and CBS was a big fat ZERO. The Super Bowl Halftime Show was the biggest platform in the world to promote yourself as an artist. The performers did not get paid. The NFL covered the expenses and production costs, which could run upwards of twenty million dollars. The benefit to Church, and others like him, would come following the Super Bowl as he released his new album and kicked off his eighth concert tour. Ticket sales and music downloads would increase significantly, resulting in the well-earned payoff.

Jones stopped the procession and pointed toward the video board over their heads. "This is the world's largest HD video display," said Jones. The massive sixty-yard side display stretched across most of the field. He continued. "There are two hundred thousand tons of concert rigging up there. The capabilities of Cowboys stadium will make this the greatest, most talked about halftime show in history."

"We'd be honored to be a part of it, Mr. Jones," said Colton. Colton looked at the inner workings of the stadium. Wires and electronics traversed the structure. *I'd hate to see their electric bill.*

# CHAPTER 3

**36 Hours**
**11:11 a.m., September 7**
**Davidson Academy**
**Nashville, Tennessee**

Alexis Ryman was settling into her sophomore year at Davidson Academy. As a freshman last year, she'd participated in most school activities available to her, but the lesson curriculum was a giant leap from middle school. Alex found herself studying for the first time and followed her interests from childhood, which included science, golf, and to a much lesser extent, cute boys.

She promised herself she'd never become a *twit*, which was Alex's designation for teenage girls who gained the attention of boys by acting ditzy, silly, and foolish. Her love of golf taught her that practice made perfect, as the old saying went. The more these girls practiced being a *twit*, the better they would become at it.

Besides, she proudly inherited her mother's good looks although Alex would never aspire to be a debutante like her mom. Alex was not shy, but she was not interested in fighting the wars that accompanied the world of high society. Her family didn't live like that, and she had no interest in it.

Unlike most of her girlfriends, Alex had an aptitude for math and science. She was not a geek per se, although her tall, lanky frame did make her appear clumsy to some. One of her friends commented that she resembled Jamie Lee Curtis, who played Laurie Strode in the movie *Halloween*. Alex wasn't sure if she was being insulted or not, so she watched the movie scene where Laurie strolled down the sidewalk in her flowered skirt, carrying her schoolbooks. *Okay, maybe she did walk a little pigeon-toed.*

As teenaged girls went, Alex was a model daughter and an honor high school student. Her grades were perfect, never a hint of trouble, and she shunned the advances of the boys who had a single purpose on their mind—sex. At fifteen, she was fully aware of the games they played, and she wouldn't fall victim to their overtures. Dates were fine and curfews were met. If you didn't like the rules, move along to someone else.

Mr. Stark, her astronomy teacher, began to write on the blackboard, causing the class to get ready for the lecture. Davidson Academy was one of the finest private schools in Nashville. Its admission requirements were stringent, and the academics were designed to prepare its students for college. High schools in the Metro Nashville system focused on conformity to rules and a set curriculum. Davidson fostered independent thinking. From her middle school days there through the present, she was taught to be an independent thinker. Students were encouraged to challenge conventional wisdom and learn *how to think* and not *what to think.*

As he finished, Stark set the chalk in the tray and pointed to the blackboard—*Solar Sleuths.* "For the first four weeks of this semester, we've covered the basics of astronomy and the physics of the universe," said Stark. Then he channeled his sci-fi hero and continued, "Adventure, excitement, a Jedi craves not these things."

The class laughed as one of the guys recognized the quote and chimed in, "But, Master Yoda, it is the lightsaber which excites me most!"

Stark continued to play along. "Young Jedis, you must unlearn what you have learned."

"Yeah!" shouted one.

"Alright!" added another.

"Okay, calm down, y'all." Stark moved to restore order. "I didn't mean that literally. The universe is vast. We needed to get an overview under your belt before we start to talk about specifics.

Today, young skulls full of mush, I will turn you into Jedi Solar Sleuths."

This piqued Alex's interest and she sat up in her seat. Stark wrote the word *SUN* on the board and circled it several times.

Alex was puzzled. Their homework assignment had nothing to do with the sun.

"It all begins here," he started. "Without the sun, there is no life on earth. Without the sun's heat and light, the earth would be a lifeless, enormous ice ball. The sun's energy warms our seas, stirs our atmosphere, generates our weather patterns, and provides the photosynthesis to grow green plant life, which is vital to produce oxygen and food on our planet."

Alex agreed. Naturally, it was fun to speculate on the topic of *are we alone?* One of the first books she read was *Contact* by Carl Sagan. She lay in bed at night, imagining herself as Ellie, and Jodie Foster, who played the character in the movie. Her imagination would wander to the massive power the sun held, and what would happen if it burned out. The risk of not using sunscreen was minor in comparison to the sun suddenly going dark.

Her mind drifted until Stark brought her back into the classroom with a question. "Alex, what causes an aurora?"

She sat up in her chair and replied, "An aurora is also called the *northern lights*. Sometimes the sun shoots out particles of energy that collide with our upper atmosphere. The result is a beautiful mix of colors near the earth's poles."

"Good start," he said. "Auroras are produced when the earth's magnetosphere is disturbed by the solar winds filled with highly charged electrons and protons."

A hand shot up from the back of the room. "Mr. Stark, why don't we see the aurora borealis where we live?"

"Good question," he replied. "Who would like to take a stab at that one?"

No one immediately answered, so Alex raised her hand.

"Okay, Alex," he said. "Obviously you're ready to be a solar sleuth. Why don't we see the aurora here?"

"For the aurora to extend this far south, the solar flare causing it would have to be very strong," she replied. "It could happen, but I don't think it's occurred in recent history."

"Very good, and you're right," praised Stark. "It hasn't happened since we've been around, but it has happened before." He turned to the blackboard and wrote *1859*, then circled it.

"In 1859, the *great geomagnetic storm*, as they called it, hit the earth. There weren't sophisticated instruments to record the magnitude of the solar flare that enveloped our northern hemisphere, but the auroras were so widespread and extraordinarily bright that they were seen as far south as Cuba and Hawaii."

"So there is hope for us, right?" asked one of the students.

"Actually, let's not hope for a repeat of the Carrington Event, as it's now called," replied Stark. "There were no electronics in 1859, but the telegraph operators certainly experienced the power of the sun. From coast to coast, telegraph wires exploded in sparks and the operators received electric shocks."

Alex raised her hand after contemplating the enormity of what Stark just said. "What would happen if a solar flare like that hit our planet today?"

Stark placed his hands in his pockets and walked through the classroom with his head down. He paused to look through the classroom's windows at the extraordinarily warm September day.

"If such a powerful burst were to hit the earth today, the energy could zap satellites, fry computer systems, and knock out our power grids. We would be welcomed back to the nineteenth century."

# CHAPTER 4

**35 Hours**
**Noon, September 7**
**Ryman Residence**
**Belle Meade, Tennessee**

"Mom, I'm comin' to Siesta Key where it's nice and cool," said Madison Ryman as she wiped the sweat from her forehead. With the cordless phone propped against her shoulder, she turned on the television, and the graphic underneath the image of Meteorologist Davis Nolan at WKRN said it all—*RECORD HEAT*. She read the closed-captioning while her mother spoke into the phone. *One hundred five degrees ... ties a record set in 1954 ... no end in sight.*

"Of course we will, Mom. I miss you too. Love you." Madison exhaled and glanced into the backyard at the rippling, crystal clear water in the pool. *No time today.* She started separating the bags of supplies picked up from Party City. The informal get-together Friday night was intended to celebrate Colton's Super Bowl success and would be attended by a couple of dozen friends, neighbors, and business associates. Bobby Bones, a longtime family friend and one of the top on-air talents at WSIX, would be there. He would provide a never-ending supply of humor.

Bones introduced Colton to Madison sixteen years ago during a music video shoot on Second Avenue. At the time, Madison was a graduate student at Lipscomb University, studying film and creative media. Before her dad passed away, he convinced her that being a debutante wouldn't pay the bills. Once the cotillions were over, it was time to get serious about her future. Lipscomb University provided her an outstanding, faith-based local university that was well respected in her chosen field—digital entertainment.

She loved producing videos. At the age of sixteen, she produced an indie film titled *Diary of a Deb*, which gained her an Independent Spirit Award nomination. She was proud of her efforts and entered college with the goal of becoming a filmmaker.

During the music video shoot, she snuck away to have lunch with Colton, and they began dating. He was everything she sought in a man, besides his incredible good looks. He was caring and compassionate. He was always honest with her. Above all, he made her laugh.

They were married in a modest ceremony at First Baptist Church in downtown Nashville and immediately started a family. Colton's career at United Talent was taking off, and she tried to continue her job as a creative director for Ruckus Films. For a while, Madison's mother helped out with Alex, but after her mom moved to Siesta Key, Madison focused her life on the things that mattered most—Colton and Alex. She never regretted that decision.

Madison focused on raising their adorable daughter and providing the *logistical support*, as she liked to call it, for Colton's social engagements. His position at United Talent required entertaining and social gatherings. At least once a month, Madison was organizing a get-together in their Belle Meade home.

Friday night, the center of attention would be on Colton rather than his more famous clients for a change. Her iPhone vibrated on the counter. It was a text from Colton.

C: Miss you!

She smiled as she responded.

M: Miss you more! Call after the concert tonight. Love!

That was all it took—a simple text to remind Madison of how much he missed her. She knew how busy Colton was, especially today, the biggest day of his career. Yet Colton was thinking of her.

The landscape service arrived and began their work. Despite the incredible heat, the primarily Hispanic crew got right to it, and the sounds of mowers could be heard immediately. It was just another day.

# CHAPTER 5

**32 Hours**
**3:00 p.m., September 7**
**Davidson Academy**
**Nashville, Tennessee**

Madison wheeled the Chevy Suburban toward the circle drive in front of Davidson Academy and patiently waited as other parents picked up their kids. Alex had a golf match that afternoon, and she needed a change of clothes and her clubs. There were plenty of other schools closer to their home in Belle Meade, but Madison was willing to sacrifice her time for the sake of the best college preparatory education Alex could receive.

She turned on her SiriusXM radio to channel 161, which had resumed the simulcast of WSIX in Nashville. After a moment, she opted for the news instead and found Shepherd Smith on Fox.

*"Aurora watchers will be pleased over the next few nights as our sun heats up,"* said Smith. *"With record heat waves across the country, the last thing we need is a fired-up sun, right, Janice Dean?"*

*"That's right, Shep,"* said Dean, the Fox News meteorologist. *"As you know, I was born in Toronto, Canada, and started my career in Ottawa. Seeing the northern lights was not out of the ordinary for us. In Canada, we would forecast the weather here on earth, but we would also provide our viewers a space weather forecast based upon solar activity. I bet you didn't realize I wore so many hats, did you?"*

*"I did not,"* replied Smith. *"Folks, this is why they call her Janice Dean the Weather Queen."*

*"And don't you forget it, Shep. From what I've seen, this solar event should create some incredible light displays along our northern border states and well into*

21

*Maine. That's pretty rare, Shep, and is an indicator of the potential strength of the solar flares emanating from the sun right now."*

*"Thank you, Janice. Keep us posted. In any event, not to worry, folks. The Canadians will get the pretty light show and we'll get more blistering heat. Same old, same old."*

Alex tapped on the window. Madison was lost in thought and didn't realize her daughter was there, causing her to jump a little. She fumbled for the lock switch and relocked the doors before finally unlocking them.

"Hey, Mom, it was a little warm out there," said Alex as she threw her book bag in the back seat. Alex immediately adjusted the air-conditioning vents, stealing all the cold air for her face.

Madison pulled out of line and made her way to the exit of the parking lot. "Sorry, honey. I was off in zuzu land for a minute. Where are we headed?"

"We're playin' at Hillwood today," replied Alex; then she added, "I'm pretty excited about it. Their home course was where the U.S. Senior Women's Open was held this summer."

"Cool. You can compare your scores to theirs and see how they stack up."

"Different tees, Mom," replied Alex.

Madison wasn't sure what that meant, so she shrugged it off. "I'll make a few stops while I wait. There may be some things I missed for the party Friday night."

Alex studied her phone for a moment as she received a Snapchat notification. Her thumbs rapidly tapped a response. Madison was still mastering *Bragbook* and her latest passion, Instagram. She liked Instagram better because the users were friendlier. On Facebook, everybody seemed mad about something. She hated the negativity and the bullies.

"Are you nervous about the party?" asked Alex, continuing to multitask, as young people called only paying half-attention to the person they were talking to. "You seemed like you were in a trance."

"No, I was just listening to the news. They were talking about solar flares and auroras."

Alex abandoned her socializing and immediately turned to her mother. "Really? That's what we discussed in Mr. Stark's class today."

"Apparently, there's a potential for a solar flare that will create an aurora as far south as Maine. They didn't act like it was a big deal, but I found it odd that it was being discussed on the news at all. I mean, don't we have more important things going on in the world besides auroras?"

"It could be important, Mom," said Alex.

Madison pressed her thumb on the steering wheel volume control and turned up the volume on the radio. Fox had two people yelling at each other about politics. *Angry.*

"Try CNN," she said to Alex, who pushed the preset on the dashboard. Madison turned up the volume further.

"*… an electromagnetic surge from a solar storm is a realistic threat. Scientists expect a major solar storm to reach the earth about once a century.*"

"*Didn't we have a near-miss in 2012?*" the CNN host asked.

"*Yes. In fact, my colleagues submitted an analysis of this solar event to* Scientific American *magazine. It took nearly two years for the government to release the full details of what could have been the worst solar storm in our history.*"

"*Was it a close call?*"

"*The coronal mass ejection that occurred in July 2012 sent eighty billion pounds of energized particles toward our planet at the speed of several million miles per hour. Luckily it barely missed Earth. Had it occurred just one week earlier, our planet would have taken a direct hit.*"

"*What would that mean in real terms?*" the host asked.

"*Given our current state of readiness, we'd still be picking up the pieces,*" the guest replied.

"*How bad?*"

"*A major solar storm containing X-class flares sends these blobs of particles toward the earth, which carry their own magnetic field. These missile-like groups of matter are capable of opening a gate in the earth's magnetic field, allowing the energetic particles to enter the atmosphere and send currents all the way down to the planet's surface. They can induce currents in the electrical grid, overheat transformers, and cause them to fail. These enormous transformers that are part of*" *our power grid can take months or years to replace. You can't exactly buy another one at Home Depot."*

"That explains it," said Alex as she adjusted the volume.

"Explains what?" asked Madison as she entered the iron gates at Hillwood Country Club.

"Today, Mr. Stark completely abandoned our lesson plan. The homework assignment from last night had nothing to do with the sun and solar flares. He joked about the change of subject, but Mr. Stark really focused on the sun and its potential for danger."

"Do you think he knows something?"

"Maybe," replied Alex. "He made all of us download an app on our phones today. It's called FlareAware."

"What's it for?" Madison put the truck into park near the clubhouse entrance. Golfers were milling about, but she didn't see any of the Davidson Academy team.

"The app provides you up-to-the-minute reports on the sun's activity. Most of the time, it doesn't send you any alerts. But when a major eruption occurs, they send out phone voice mails and text alerts. FlareAware gives you real-time warnings where the news does not."

Madison popped the rear hatch to help Alex get her gear together. The Fox report had downplayed the potential of the solar storm. *Why? Are they hiding something, or are they protecting us from ourselves?*

# CHAPTER 6

**31 Hours**
**4:21 p.m., September 7**
**West End Avenue**
**Nashville, Tennessee**

Madison tried to put the thoughts of solar Armageddon out of her mind. If they faced a significant danger, the government would tell them about it. She walked into Barnes & Noble to grab a Starbucks and kill some time. While she enjoyed reading on her Kindle, she still liked the touch and feel of magazines. She grabbed her coffee and made her way to the magazine rack.

A sizable group of people crowded around a table where an author was conducting a book signing. The people waiting in line didn't look like the *tweed jacket and leather elbow patch* Vandy crowd. Most wore some form of camouflaged hunting clothing. There were babies on hips and young children squirming by their parent's side. Madison decided to get a closer look.

The author was signing books and chatting up his readers. "How would you like me to address it?" he asked.

"My name is Lesley Prentice Henry. That's spelled L-E-S-L-E-Y. You can skip the Prentice part."

"Okay, Lesley," the author said, laughing. He looked up at her under the bill of his camouflaged hat, which had a lightning bolt streaked across the front. "Are you a prepper?"

"We're working on it," she replied. Then she added, seemingly embarrassed, "It's overwhelming and expensive."

"I understand," he said. He stopped writing and focused his attention on her. "I tell everybody to concentrate on the simple things, namely beans, Band-Aids, and bullets. In the back of my book, you'll find an appendix with a detailed checklist and links to my website. Take baby steps, Lesley. If you ever have any questions, just email me. I'd be glad to help."

"Well, thank you, sir, for your advice," she said. "May I ask one more question?"

"Of course," he said, smiling to the next person in line as if to apologize for the delay. Those waiting didn't seem to mind.

"You've written a lot of books about prepping," she started. "What do you fear the most?"

The author laughed. "Great question. First of all, I don't fear anything. *Why?* Because my wife and I are ready for every potential scenario. That said, I believe the biggest threat our nation faces is any catastrophic event that results in a collapse of our critical infrastructure."

"Like what?" asked the next person in line.

"Our country faces many threats, both natural and man-made. Any of these could cause our power grid to go dark, and the result would be societal and economic collapse."

"What's most likely?" Lesley pressed him for more information.

"Cyber attack is at the top of my list," the author replied. "The attack could come from within or without our nation's borders. It could be orchestrated by a nation like Russia, a terrorist group like ISIS, or a pimple-faced kid in his momma's basement. Properly implemented, a cyber attack on just nine key substations across the country could cause a cascading effect of grid failures nationwide."

"You mentioned natural threats. Do you mean like hurricanes?"

"Not really, although I believe it's just part of being a responsible adult to prep for natural disasters like hurricanes and tornados," the author replied. "In my opinion, the biggest natural threat we face comes from our sun in the form of a massive solar flare. Like a cyber attack or a nuclear-delivered electromagnetic pulse, a solar flare has the potential to destroy the grid as well. We live in an interconnected world full of tiny circuits and electronics. These devices are not capable of absorbing the tremendous influx of energy that is generated by a major geomagnetic storm. With little warning, we could be thrown back into the 1800s."

"Gee, thank you, I guess." The woman chuckled. "I mean, thanks for signing the book for me."

"You're welcome," he replied, and then added, "Don't be afraid, Lesley. Be ready."

Madison had never heard the term *prepper* before. She certainly didn't know how it related to beans and bullets. She walked toward the magazines, searching for *Us Weekly*, and decided to look up the definition of a prepper. Google happily obliged with a result.

A person who believes a catastrophic disaster or emergency is likely to occur in the future and makes active preparations for it, typically by stockpiling food, ammunition, and other supplies.

Okay, she thought. Being a prepper sounded like something a grown-up Boy Scout might do.

She scrolled through some of the other search results provided by Google. Websites like the Atlantic Monthly, the NY Times, and Mother Jones demeaned preppers as being conspiracy theorists, part of the tinfoil hat crowd, and generally fanatical.

She took another glance at the line, which had grown longer, and then she glanced back to the author. Maybe these people were onto something. He certainly didn't look like a wackadoo.

# CHAPTER 7

**27 Hours**
**8:00 p.m., September 7**
**ALMA**
**Atacama, Chile**

Dr. Stanford walked through the rows of cubicles and monitors in the ALMA control room. A few personnel were monitoring the JUNO spacecraft, which was entering the atmosphere of Jupiter. The project, launched five years ago, was designed to study the formation of Jupiter's gravity and magnetic fields, as well as it evolution. The data received from JUNO about the gas giant could provide valuable insight into the solar system.

"We have another one, Dr. Stanford," announced one of the JAO Team.

"Talk to me."

"It's odd, ma'am," he replied. "This appears to be another C-class flare."

"What are the details?" she asked.

"This was released from the lower right quadrant of AR3222. It peaked approximately two hours ago. Preliminary data indicates a moderate C3.2 solar flare."

"What about speed?" she asked.

"It emanated as a steady, relatively faint, but asymmetrical, full halo coronal mass ejection. It is fairly slow, only measuring about four hundred kilometers per second."

"That's barely faster than the background solar wind," quipped Dr. Stanford.

She was puzzled by this active region. The coronal hole at the heart of AR3222 was massive, yet it hadn't produced even a minor disturbance. Throughout the day, the JAO Team reported several inconsequential C-class solar flares from the remainder of the region.

"Do we call it in?" asked the analyst, interrupting her thoughts.

"Like the C-flare from yesterday, I doubt there will be any geomagnetic storming from this event due to the slow speed of the CME. Just keep monitoring, and please, don't get lulled into a false sense of security."

Dr. Stanford needed some air. The sun would be setting over the western edge of the Andes and would be a beautiful sight. At the end of most days, she would head home, only to renew her monitoring in the morning. Tonight, she planned to sleep on the sofa in her cramped office.

She walked into the rapidly cooling night air. The temperatures rose well into the nineties by late afternoon, but would be in the low thirties within hours.

Ordinarily, watching the sunset would calm her. People paid big bucks to travel to the beach, dig their toes in the sand, and watch the ball of fire sink into the ocean. To most, it was comforting that the sun would be back the next day, bringing with it light and life. As the sun began to fall over the westernmost peaks into the horizon of the Pacific Ocean, she talked to it.

Dr. Stanford was skeptical. "What are you up to? I feel like you're waiting for something." She stared as the fireball slowly disappeared. She brushed the hair out of her face and tucked it behind her ears.

She stared at the dormant volcanoes that blended into the landscape of the Andes Mountains. These sleeping giants would roar to life again someday. The molten lava and gasses of a volcano would increase in pressure until it was vented, resulting in an eruption.

The sun worked on the same principle, although no lava was involved. The hot gasses and ionized particles swelled until the plasma was released. A chill ran over her body, and she unconsciously hugged herself, still staring at the bright orange star as it disappeared over the Andes. Then it dawned on her.

"It's building."

# CHAPTER 8

**27 Hours**
**8:00 p.m., September 7**
**American Airlines Center**
**Dallas**

Outside of the American Airlines Center was a sign containing the letters—VIP. Fans of the NBA's Dallas Mavericks and the NHL's Dallas Stars walked past the dedicated entrance every game, but few of them got to enter the Lexus Garage allowing access to the premium seating. Admission to the luxury suites didn't just mean you got to separate yourself from the rest of the madness that accompanied a large-scale concert like tonight's. The perks went further than that. Attendees in the luxury suites got specialty foods and cocktails, concierge-level service, private restrooms, and features including multiple HDTV screens streaming the concert as well as any channel available on DirecTV.

Colton was beginning to enjoy the perks of his status as one of the premier talent agents in the nation. Soon, he would be sought by promoters of events seeking access to his client base, as opposed to the other way around.

The concert was in full swing, but most of the guests of Jerry Jones engaged in conversation and drinks. Joining them tonight in the luxury suite were Rudy Gatlin of the Gatlin Brothers, Kelly Clarkson of *American Idol* fame, and Colby Donaldson, who became known for his runner-up appearance on the second season of *Survivor* on CBS. He subsequently appeared on the *Survivor* reality show in two more seasons.

"Pretty incredible, don't you think?" said Donaldson to Colton.

Colton took another bite of a buffalo chicken sandwich and nodded with his mouth full. "Yeah, it is," he replied, swallowing fast. "I saw a Nashville Stars game in one of their suites, but the level of luxury wasn't close to this. While walking through the AA concourse, I recognized a lot of local celebrities." Despite his career, Colton, who had a humble upbringing, was still starstruck at times.

Donaldson put down his Bud Light and grabbed another one out of the refrigerator. "Want one?" he asked Colton.

"No, thanks, this IBC is fine." Colton didn't drink beer, opting instead for his longtime favorite *roost beer*, as he'd called it since childhood. "Do you come up here often?"

"This is my first time in Mr. Jones's suite. I've been providing members of his family some firearms training."

"I've caught a couple of episodes of *Top Shot*," said Colton. "Six years is a pretty good run."

"Thanks," smiled Donaldson with a tip of his beer. "I was thrilled with the opportunity that the History Channel gave me. Between the various challenges and the variety of contestants, I have the chance to provide decent entertainment for their viewers while informing people about the safe use of firearms at the same time."

Colton polished off his sandwich and chased it with the last of his IBC. He thought about the raging debate in America over the ownership of guns and the Second Amendment. Colton believed in and supported the Constitutional right to bear arms. He was also convinced that guns didn't kill people but, rather, people killed people. Like most Americans, however, he hated to read about mass shootings and the deaths that resulted. As an emotional issue, the debate created a political divide in the country, which Colton tried to avoid. Politics and business didn't mix very well.

"Well, congrats, Colby," said Colton. "You've really parlayed your appearance on *Survivor* into something great. Your success takes initiative, which can't be taught in school. Keep it rollin'!"

"I will. It's nice to meet you," said Donaldson, who suddenly turned his attention to the television monitor showing CNN.

"Dadgummit! I'm supposed to fly to Anchorage in the morning for filming."

The monitor contained closed-captioning of a reporter discussing a breaking news announcement from the FAA. Colton pushed his way past the overstuffed leather chairs to get a better look at the details from the report.

CNN's headline read *Geomagnetic Storm Warning*. Colton considered turning up the volume to hear the details, but only he and Donaldson were watching. The closed caption would have to suffice.

*"The FAA, after receiving reports from NOAA, has redirected dozens of flights that were routed from Alaska to some of the northernmost regions of Canada. All flights scheduled to fly across the north pole have been rerouted.*

*"NOAA advised the FAA that one of its satellites witnessed an ultraviolet flash from a solar eruption and data indicated it to be a C-class solar flare. Although relatively common, the FAA felt it was necessary to reroute the flights out of an abundance of precaution.*

*"Stay tuned to CNN for further updates."*

A voice interrupted Colton and Donaldson as they watched the report. "We knew that some of the Air Canada flights would be affected by this," said Martin Hart, a sitting member of the American Airlines board of directors and also a guest of Jerry Jones. "Several airlines didn't fly polar routes today, and we adjusted the flight pattern of a few of our flights as well."

Colton turned to greet the man. "I'm Colton Ryman," he said, extending his hand.

"Marty Hart, I'm on the board of AA." He shook Colton's hand. "How're you, Colby?"

"Fine, sir," replied Donaldson as the men exchanged handshakes. "Will my flight to Anchorage be affected?"

"Probably not. We'll take a more southerly route on most flights as we continue to monitor the situation. These solar flares happen all the time. Most of them are G1 or G2 storms which usually accompany a C-class solar flare like this one. But even the G2s can impact low Earth satellites, radio comms, and cause navigation issues. We adjust accordingly."

"That's good," said Donaldson. "I was supposed to fly out this morning but chose to hang out with you guys. My friends at Pilgrim Studios would turn me into a range target if I missed that flight." The men laughed, but Colton turned his attention back to the television monitor.

The advisory scrolled across the bottom of the screen. He was due to fly home on Friday morning after the football game, and he missed his girls. Surely this solar flare would be long gone by then.

# CHAPTER 9

**27 Hours**
**8:00 p.m., September 7**
**Ryman Residence**
**Belle Meade, Tennessee**

Madison scrolled down the iPad through her Facebook news feed and mindlessly clicked the like button on her friends' posts. Her mind was elsewhere, and Madison probably would have chastised herself for *liking* the post of her neighbor who announced the loss of her father. *Liking* a post concerning the death of a loved one seemed like bad form without some accompanying comment of support.

She paused the television while waiting for Alex. They both enjoyed watching *Big Brother* on CBS, and tonight's episode was going to reveal a new twist in the final weeks of this season. Finally, growing impatient, she yelled upstairs for Alex.

"Hey, are you finished with your homework?" Madison hated yelling through the house. Maybe she should've sent her daughter a text message. She laughed to herself at how lazy Americans had become.

"Yes, Mom," Alex hollered back, with a dose of teenage girl sarcasm. "I'll be there in a minute."

Madison switched her iPad to Instagram and repeatedly double-tapped the *heart* button, indicating her approval of a particular image. She just wasn't into it, so she set down her iPad and headed up the winding staircase to Alex's bedroom. Their home was larger than the three of them needed. Besides the obligatory guest bedroom, they could have easily eliminated the formal living room, which gathered dust, and the other two upstairs bedrooms, which contained older,

34

space-filling furniture.

The upstairs was Alex's domain. Her room looked like a page out of the Pottery Barn Teen catalog. Alex was not a girly-girl. As she got older, her styles gravitated to classic designs—very Hamptons. White and blues were prevalent in the furnishings. Paintings of famous oceanfront golf courses like Pebble Beach and Mauna Kea in Hawaii provided wall coverings. There were no posters of Justin Bieber or, heaven forbid, Kanye West. Alex enjoyed music. She just didn't want to stare at it all day.

Madison entered the mysterious domain of the teenage girl and found Alex on her iMac. Expecting to see Snapchat or Periwinkle or Periscope or some such, Madison was surprised to see the scorching red sun rotating on her computer screen.

"Hey, Mom, check this out."

"Is this a new way to get a suntan?"

"Very funny," replied Alex with a roll of her eyes. "No, look at this website. It's called SolarMonitor.org."

Madison laughed to herself as she pulled up a chair. *Most parents are worried about their kids being propositioned by pedophiles online. My kid is watching the sun rotate.* Madison thought there could be a bumper sticker concept in all of this.

"Tell me about it," said Madison.

"This was one of the websites Mr. Stark told us about in class today. The other two were SpaceWeather.com and SpaceWeatherLive.com. You can learn so much about the sun from these sites." Alex navigated through the web pages and showed Madison the various tools available.

She stopped on the image revealing the sun in its present status. Using this particular satellite view, the sun appeared to be a variety of shades of purple with a fainter halo protruding from its surface.

"This is the sun right now as it faces the earth," said Alex.

"Is this normal?"

"Yes. The sun has good days and bad days. On the good days, there is very little activity, which means no solar flares." Alex pointed to the monitor and ran her fingers across the bottom pointing to the lower half of the sun. "See here. NOAA states there are no active regions in this view. Active regions are areas for solar flare potential."

"Okay. This is good, right?" asked Madison.

"Oh, this is good," started Alex. "But this—not so much." She navigated the cursor to a link marked *far side*.

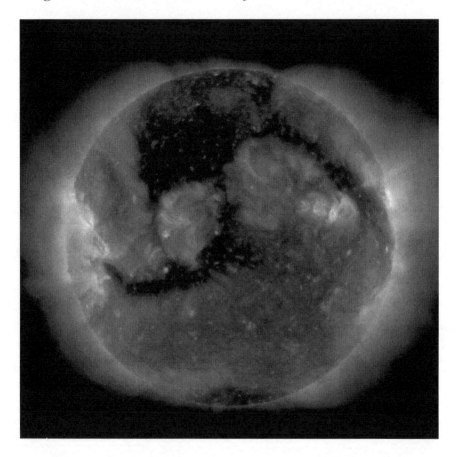

"Wow," exclaimed Madison. "What happened to it?"

"Mom, this is the far side of the sun, which will be rotating back around and pointed at us soon," Alex explained. She ran her fingers around the massive void encompassing the top half of the sun. "Do you see this? This is a coronal hole. A coronal hole produces solar flares."

"Are they always this big?"

"I don't think so, Mom," replied Alex. Alex reached into her book bag and pulled out a physical science book. She turned to the section on space sciences and found the image she was looking for. She handed the book to her Mom and pointed at the textbook image. "This is a coronal hole capable of producing an X-class solar flare."

Madison took the book out of her daughter's hands and studied it, thumbing the pages back and forth. The caption read that the coronal hole depicted in the textbook version created an X3 solar flare. Madison held the book next to the monitor to look at the similarities of the two images.

"See, Mom," started Alex. "There's no comparison. If the picture of the sun in my book produced an X3-class flare, imagine what this coronal hole, which is twenty times larger, might produce?"

"What's the next larger flare after an X?"

"There isn't one. X is the last letter and the largest of the classes. An X2 is twice as powerful as an X1. An X5, considered huge, is five times larger than an X1, and so on. The largest on record is an X28 that occurred in 2003."

Madison continued to study the two images. "Alex, the current sun image is easily twenty times larger than your textbook image."

"Yes, twenty times an X3," said Alex.

"What's twenty times three?" asked Madison, who was beginning to understand the magnitude of this.

"It's still sixty, Mom," replied Alex. "That could make an X60."

Madison dropped the book with a loud thud on the hardwood floor.

# CHAPTER 10

**26 Hours**
**9:00 p.m., September 7**
**Space Weather Prediction Center**
**Boulder, Colorado**

"Our star—the Sun—is a bubbling, boiling ball of fire," explained the tour guide to a group of middle-school-age kids from Salt Lake City. She was walking along the concourse, pointing to a series of high-definition images on the walls. She stopped and directed the group's attention to the latest imagery from SOHO—the Solar and Heliospheric Observatory. "The Sun constantly belches out great clouds of hot gas. This gas is all charged up with electricity, too. This stuff travels at astounding speeds, some of it right toward Earth!"

The predominantly pre-teen group of children burst out in giggles after hearing the words *belch* and *gas* in the same sentence. Their teacher, who stifled a smile, admonished them to settle down.

"What happens if it hits Earth?" asked a composed young man from the group.

"Thank goodness Earth's magnetic field and our atmosphere protects us from most of the blast," she replied, pointing at a colorful image of Earth and the invisible magnetic lines of force, which exit near the south pole and re-enter near the north pole. The guide ignored a few more giggles. "Otherwise, the Sun's weather would become our weather. Yikes, right?"

The SWPC tour guide had a way of using voice inflection to create a sense of drama. If you didn't know better, you'd think she was trying to scare the children. This was her last tour of the day, and it was specially arranged for the early evening hour by a congressman's office. *A nighttime tour deserved a little extra drama.*

She continued along the corridor, explaining the impact of solar winds, how the northern lights were created, and what happened when the sun got *restless*.

"Watch this animated GIF of the sun during a period of restlessness," she started. The graphic image of the July 14, 2000, Bastille Day eruption played a constant, looping animation of the full-halo X5.7 flare, which subsequently caused an S3 radiation storm.

"Wow!" said one of the kids.

"Here it comes," exclaimed the tour guide gleefully. "See these sudden, intense hiccups and burps? These are called solar flares and coronal mass ejections."

"The sun has solar indigestion!" The children's teacher laughed, but for once, the kids were focused on the presentation.

"I guess you could say that," added the tour guide. "But the effects of these types of space weather events are not so pretty. When all of these X-rays and charged particles reach Earth, they can cause trouble."

The children stopped talking amongst themselves and turned their attention to the guide.

"Like what?" asked one child with trepidation.

"Bad space weather can interrupt radio signals. It can damage satellites. Ships at sea may not be able to use their navigation equipment. Their two-way radios may not work. And sometimes, the power of the sun can cause damage to the electrical systems that bring power to our homes."

"Like a blackout?"

"That's right," she replied. "That's why the SWPC—the Space Weather Prediction Center—is so important. Just as we need early warnings about hurricanes, tornadoes, and other bad weather, having early warnings of bad space weather helps us keep damage from solar flares to a minimum."

She led the class down a corridor and through a double set of doors. The group entered a soundproof, glass-enclosed auditorium overlooking the scientists inside the Space Weather Forecast Office of the SWPC. Monitors provided multiple views of space and the sun. Some screens provided external views of orbiting satellites, and there was a constant stream of data and numbers being produced on the large displays in the center of the room.

The kids settled into the theater-style seating, and the tour guide was about to continue her presentation when one of the children spoke first.

"Are those two men going to fight?"

*****

"We can't keep a lid on this!" said one of the space forecasters as he slammed down a pile of time-lapse photos of the sun.

"You don't think I know that," replied his adversary, who was also his superior. "But it hasn't done anything yet. How do I justify raising an unprecedented threat awareness based upon no track record?" The two scientists stared at each other, hands on hips, with only a cluster of computer monitors separating them. All eyes were on them, including the visiting schoolkids in the gallery.

The SPWC Forecast Center was jointly operated by NOAA and the U.S. Air Force. Its primary responsibility was to provide global warnings for disturbances that could affect people and equipment impacted by everything from solar flares to asteroids. The services they provide influenced the decision-making processes of NASA, the armed services, the FAA, the Department of Transportation, and FERC—the Federal Energy Regulatory Commission, which regulated the power grid.

The men remained in a standoff until the scientist, after deliberately pounding the keyboard of his computer, brought the far-side image of the sun on all the large wall-mounted monitors. On display was the most recent image indicating the massive coronal hole that had formed on the northern hemisphere of the sun.

The space weather forecaster who raised the alarm took off his glasses and walked around the room. He studied the faces of his co-workers.

"Do you think *that* will disappear overnight? Seriously?" he asked sarcastically while pointing toward the monitors.

The sun slowly, almost imperceptibly, rotated on the screen as it fluxed and oscillated. It looked like a gigantic fusion reactor preparing to create a massive release of energy.

The senior scientist broke the silence. "Give me the current forecast—best available estimate."

The space weather forecasters all turned their attention back to their stations, and the keyboards began to clatter. The monitors changed as each of the forecast models were determined.

"First up, what's the radio blackout prediction at zero hour," asked the senior scientist.

"R5, extreme—a complete high-frequency radio blackout on the entire sunlit side of Earth, lasting for hours, if not days. Airline travel will need to be halted, and oceangoing vessels will need to be notified well in advance."

"Radiation?"

"Yes, sir. Our scale predicts *extreme* as well. An S5 radiation storm is likely. All aircraft passengers will be exposed to radiation at high altitudes. NASA should abort any EVA, extravehicular activity. Many satellites will be rendered useless, in some cases permanently."

The senior scientist rubbed his temples and walked around the room. He glanced up at the observation auditorium and noticed the schoolkids for the first time. None of them were speaking and the tour guide was staring back at him. He tried not to show any concern and managed a smile as he turned back to his team.

"Call out the G-scale effects."

"Sir, I'm predicting a geomagnetic storm of the highest level, a G5. We are predicting a massive voltage control failure across all interconnected power grids. Transformers will experience damage resulting in blackouts and, potentially, collapse."

"ETA?"

"We predict the initial impact in higher latitudes will be felt within twenty hours. At that time, there is the potential for widespread voltage control problems, and some protective systems will mistakenly trip out key assets from the grid. NASA will need to be advised that unavoidable radiation hazards to their astronauts will be experienced. Likewise, passengers in high-flying aircraft may be exposed to radiation. Radio blackouts will become more prevalent."

"What's the zero hour?" he asked as he slumped in his chair and prepared to pick up the receiver for the requisite call to Kathryn Sullivan, the Under Secretary of Commerce who acted as the administrator of NOAA.

"Sir, we are forecasting full impact to Earth in approximately twenty-four hours as an X58 solar event."

# CHAPTER 11

**25 Hours**
**10:17 p.m., September 7**
**Ryman Residence**
**Belle Meade, Tennessee**

"Here it is, Mom," said Alex as she navigated the cursor onto the YouTube channel of Dr. Andrea Stanford. Using the moniker Space Weather Woman, she provided constant updates on her website and via YouTube presentations. She'd been featured in numerous television documentaries and on The Weather Channel. "Dr. Stanford just uploaded it. Look at all of the views already!"

"Does that read four thousand?" asked Madison, pointing at the bottom of the computer monitor. "And when was it uploaded?"

"Yes, Mom. She uploaded it seven minutes ago and it's going viral. Let's watch it."

Alex increased the volume on her speakers and used the cursor to hit the play icon on the screen. Dr. Stanford came to life. She was pointing to a newspaper headline image, which read *Minivan destroyed after GPS leads driver onto MBTA tracks*. Accompanying the headline was a minivan ripped in half by a commuter train in the Boston area.

*"Now, we'll start this forecast by reminding you how important it is to pay attention to space weather. This happened a month ago when a mother and two children barely escaped alive when the car's GPS unit steered them onto the tracks in front of an oncoming train. Sadly, this event occurred while the northern hemisphere was under a G3 geomagnetic storm warning, which disrupted GPS units and radio broadcasts. Had a more public warning of this G3 event been given, the mother might not have relied upon her GPS as she did under normal solar conditions."*

Madison pulled up a chair. "My God, those poor people."

"Look, Mom, the views are approaching ten thousand."

*"From my last update, where we announced an X2.2 flare and the launch of a solar storm, we now have a new active region that has crossed the solar disk, which has been identified as AR3222. By new, however, I mean old. AR3222 has grown in size to encompass much of the Sun's northern hemisphere. This is an image of the far side taken a few moments ago. A huge dark coronal hole has formed, and this has the potential to slam Earth with some fast solar wind.*

*"We didn't get much aurora from this solar storm today, which is, frankly, puzzling. But that should change as this enormous black void rotates into Earth view on the east limb tomorrow morning.*

*"We can expect the fast solar wind to increase, and this region will most likely launch solar storms in the next twelve hours. Regular viewers of my forecast know that I'm not an alarmist. My primary goal is to provide you the latest space weather forecast so you can prepare accordingly. In the past, our government agencies have chosen not to inform you of the consequences of significant solar activity. I believe you are capable of making an informed decision.*

*"There is a very strong possibility of extreme solar weather, so please take my forecast into consideration to determine how that might impact your day tomorrow. Outside of that, expect to have some amazing auroras stretching as far south as Arizona, Louisiana, and Florida. So aurora watchers, look at the skies tomorrow evening and cross your fingers that this will be a wonderful display of colors and nothing more. I'm Andrea Stanford. Thank you for watching."*

"Alex, what do you—" Madison began to ask before Alex interrupted her. Alex pounded furiously on her keyboard—quickly navigating between Google search results and various websites.

"Mr. Stark said something today and I want to look it up. There! Look at this." Alex pointed to an article about the 1859 Carrington Event. "Here, Mom."

Madison read the article aloud. "What Carrington saw through his telescope was a white-light solar flare, a magnetic explosion on the sun. Before dawn the next day, skies all over the planet erupted in red, green, and purple auroras so brilliant that newspapers could be read as easily as in daylight. Indeed, stunning auroras pulsated at near tropical latitudes over Cuba, the Bahamas, Jamaica, and Hawaii."

"See, Mom. Dr. Stanford said the aurora could be seen tomorrow night in Florida. That's almost Cuba!"

Madison read more of the article before catching her breath. Alex was obviously excited about this. But being excited about some colorful skies was far different from predicting the end of the world as we know it.

"Listen, Alex. I understand your interest in all of this. It does sound exciting to see the aurora here in Nashville. I've never seen the northern lights myself."

"Mom!" exclaimed Alex as she jumped out of her chair. "I don't care about the pretty lights. Who cares about the pretty lights? A solar flare this big could cause a massive blackout. *Pretty lights?* How about *no lights?*"

Madison was concerned about her daughter's highly charged mental state. If you read enough on the Internet, you'd go around wearing a suit of armor, if you even left the house at all.

"Alex, let's see how this develops. We can see what the news tells us in the morning."

"Mom," Alex protested, "the news won't tell us anything because the government won't tell the news anything. Dad always says the government lies to us. They're probably lying now." Alex stood defiantly staring down at her mother.

"Honey"—Madison rose to her feet in an attempt to calm her daughter down—"the government is aware of this situation if Dr. Stanford knows about it. If we're threatened in some way, I'm sure the government will tell us what to do."

The phone rang, interrupting the debate. Madison checked the caller id. It was Colton, *thank God.*

"Hi, darlin'!" answered Madison, showing her genuine appreciation for the call. She didn't like to argue with Alex. "How was the concert?"

Colton provided her the details of his day in Dallas. Madison listened dutifully and interjected a comment here and there. She was still on edge over her conversation with Alex, who paced the floor impatiently. Madison touched Alex on the shoulder in an attempt to calm the tenseness between them, but Alex responded verbally.

"Mom, are you gonna tell him?" she asked.

Madison nodded and raised a finger to her lips. This didn't go over well with Alex, who didn't like to be shushed.

"Mom, please," she pleaded.

"Yes, Alex is still up. I'll put you on the speaker."

Madison gave the handset to Alex who immediately began to talk.

"Daddy, you need to come home. Are there any flights tonight?"

"Alex, what's wrong? Madison?" Colton asked over the phone loud enough for Madison to here.

Madison took the phone back from Alex and set it on the computer desk after hitting the speaker button. She took a seat and motioned for Alex to do the same.

"Honey, there are some news and internet reports that the sun is acting up and might cause a solar flare," started Madison. "Alex learned about them in school today, and coincidentally, the sun is brewing one up. But they happen all the time, and I'm sure there's nothing to—"

"It's gonna be massive, Daddy," interrupted Alex. "I've been online all night. This could be the biggest in history."

Colton relayed his conversation with the American Airlines executive tonight. He explained to Alex that these solar flares were common and didn't affect them in the south.

Alex, who had now calmed down out of resignation rather than compliance, announced that she was tired and was going to bed. She and Colton said her good-byes, and Madison took the phone with her downstairs. They'd have to watch *Big Brother* tomorrow night.

"Colton, she's worked up, that's all," started Madison after she was out of listening distance from Alex's room. "You know how she gets passionate about certain topics. Today, it's solar flares. Tomorrow, it'll be whether global warming is a hoax. You've raised quite the conservative, you know."

Colton, still on speakerphone, replied, "We've both raised a rabble-rouser!"

"That kind of activity came from your side of the family, Mr. Ryman!"

"I love you, Maddie. I appreciate Alex's concern. But tomorrow is a big day. We have the final meeting with the lawyers in the morning, and then tomorrow night is the Cowboys home opener on Thursday Night football. There'll be a big production about the Super Bowl lineup during halftime. You know what I mean."

"I know, honey. Alex will be fine. This kind of stuff floats around the Internet all the time. Tomorrow night is the announcement, you'll fly home Friday morning, and we'll have the party Friday night. Life goes on, right?"

"Yup."

# CHAPTER 12

**19 Hours**
**4:23 a.m., September 8**
**9:23 a.m. Coordinated Universal Time (UTC)**
**The Sun**

The sun has no surface per se. It's a huge sphere of glowing gasses in a constant state of flux. At its core, immense gravitational pulls produce unfathomable pressure and temperature, which can reach twenty-seven million degrees Fahrenheit. As a result, the incredible heat causes hydrogen atoms to be compressed and fused together, creating helium. The sun, and other stars like it, is the perfect nuclear fusion reactor.

The universe's consummate source of energy is always producing massive amounts of energy. This energy emanates outward toward the sun's photosphere, the lowest of its three primary layers. As this energy passes through this radiative zone, the temperature of this energy decreases by several million degrees, and, as a result, light is formed.

In the last forty-eight hours, the Sun's magnetic field bloated, and it encroached upon the photosphere. These powerful magnetic fields created sunspots in the outer atmosphere of the sun. To observers in the universe, these sunspots appear to be dark because they're cooler than the surrounding areas of the sun's photosphere. But cooler does not mean better in this instance.

The dark area of the sunspot is called the umbra. The umbra can vary in size based on the power of the magnetic field. The Sun, and stars like it, are unique because the interior and exterior rotate separately. Over time, all that messy and uneven movement twists and distorts the sun's magnetic field in the same way your bedcovers get wrinkled and bunched up when you toss and turn in your sleep.

For several days, the sun had been restless. Without conscience, the sun determined enough was enough. Its magnetic field began to wind up into a twisted mess and push its way from the sun's core.

The magnetic field's expansion into the photosphere was enormous. The magnetism build up was so intense that it inhibited the flow of hot gasses from the sun's interior to its surface.

It was powerful. It was unsustainable. It would be described as the largest in recorded history.

The magnetic field lines from the sun's interior burst through the sunspot, twisting to the point of snapping—like a rubber band wound too tight. When they snapped, they linked up again to form a new shape, but not before releasing enormous amounts of stored energy into the sun's outermost atmosphere, the corona.

The sun erupted, creating a solar flare that heated the surrounding gas to one hundred eighty million degrees. Subatomic particles of radiation in the form of ultraviolet, gamma, and X-rays spewed into space at near light-speed.

Eight minutes after the solar flare released from the Sun, Earth's atmosphere absorbed the initial radiation pulse. The pulse produced extra ions and electrons, causing the planet's atmosphere to puff out. As Earth's atmosphere expanded, there was a drag on satellites, causing disruptions in radio and GPS signals.

But the worst was yet to come.

Today, the sun had another gift—a coronal mass ejection, or CME. The coronal hole in its northern hemisphere was incapable of containing the plasma burst emanating from the sun's interior. Billions of tons of plasma were flung into space en masse. These huge bubbles of matter were rushing towards Earth, but at a much slower pace than the solar flare. At several million miles per hour, the CME could take less than a day to impact Earth.

On this day, at this hour, the CME boosted the speed of the solar wind as it approached Earth. As it traveled through space, it created a shockwave of energized protons. The shockwave would catapult itself into Earth's magnetic shield, and the protons would stream down on the north and south poles.

The wave of energy was much larger than Earth. It was aiming for the bull's-eye. It wouldn't miss.

The resulting geomagnetic storm produced dangerous currents in the atmosphere analogous to a moving bar magnet raising currents in a coil of wire. When the CME hit Earth's magnetic field, it created a rapid oscillating effect. The powerful currents of energy passed through most conductive materials on Earth's surface—anything containing a wire, an antenna, or similar metal.

The CME would hit Earth with a force equal to a billion hydrogen bombs.

It's happened before.

It will happen again—at Zero Hour.

# CHAPTER 13

**16 Hours**
**7:13 a.m., September 8**
**Ryman Residence**
**Belle Meade, Tennessee**

Madison served Alex a bowl of oatmeal topped with fresh strawberries and bananas. NewsChannel5 was streaming live on a monitor in the kitchen. There had been another terrorist attack instigated by ISIS, this time in Istanbul, Turkey. Madison couldn't imagine living in a place where a terrorist could disrupt activities on a daily basis. America had seen terror since 9/11, but they consisted of random attacks in Orlando, San Bernardino and nearby Chattanooga. The media downplayed these incidents as isolated events, but as a mother, she always feared for the safety of Alex. She couldn't imagine that type of violence in Nashville.

"Alex, get your nose out of that iPad and eat your breakfast. I've got to get you to school."

Lelan Statom, the Channel 5 staff meteorologist, began his weather report, which highlighted the record heat wave. He showed video clips of heat-exhausted joggers in Centennial Park and passed-out homeless people in a makeshift camp near the Cumberland River. The unusually warm weather was expected to continue, as indicated by another video clip of the morning sun causing heat to rise off a paved asphalt road.

"Mom, listen to this," started Alex. "This is from the UK *Daily Mail*."

"The what?"

Alex quickly ate two spoonfuls of oatmeal and replied with her mouth full, still focused on the iPad. "The *Daily Mail*, Mom, from England. It's one of the top newspapers in the UK, and they always post stories online that our newspapers won't."

"Ooookay." Madison stretched out her reply. She grabbed her coffee *road cup* out of the cabinet and poured the last of the Folgers into it. She mixed in her cream and sugar as Alex explained further.

"The headline reads *SOLAR SPLASH*," she began. Alex, who was wearing her customary Davidson Academy uniform, clinked her spoon in the bowl as she polished off the remainder of the oatmeal and then pushed it away. She began reading.

"In the hours before dawn, a solar flare blasted directly toward Earth and, shortly thereafter, it caused the aurora borealis to be seen throughout the UK and into much of Germany. In the wake of the large solar storm, those in luck will see the northern lights dancing in the night sky for days to come. Forecasters announced that people who live in high-altitude locations and as far south as Portugal will be privileged to see the aurora borealis through Thursday and Friday nights, assuming it remains strong enough.

"Officials warn, however, despite the breathtaking beauty of the northern lights, scientists believe these massive geomagnetic storms can cause widespread disruptions in the use of GPS and airline travel. The Civil Aviation Authority, in conjunction with the Americans' FAA, will be releasing an advisory statement at 4:00 p.m. Greenwich Mean Time."

Madison studied her daughter as she took the empty bowl and placed it in the dishwasher. She wondered if Alex slept at all last night. This solar flare business was beginning to become an obsession.

"Alex, I understand this is getting a lot of interest in the news, but it is also a regular occurrence. The planet experiences northern lights all the time. Even that article didn't raise any alarms."

"But, Mom," Alex started, but cut off her own thought.

Madison picked up Alex's backpack and set it on the kitchen table. She gestured for the iPad and tucked it safely inside. Then she gave her daughter a reassuring smile.

"Honey, I promise to keep an eye on this situation, just like I would any other threat our family might face. Honestly, solar flares have never been on my radar before, so I want to thank you for not only bringing them to my attention, but teaching me what you know."

"I know, Mom. They can be dangerous. We're not ready for something like this, and Daddy's in Texas. What if his flight is canceled or something?"

Madison flipped off the kitchen lights and turned off the television monitor. She led Alex out of the kitchen and opened the side door, where they were greeted with a rush of hot air. *This is ridiculous for September.*

# CHAPTER 14

**15 Hours**
**8:00 a.m., September 8**
**White House Situation Room**
**Washington, DC**

David Lemmon had been friends with NOAA's Administrator Kathryn Sullivan for over thirty years. As he reached retirement, he found himself performing ceremonial duties on behalf of Secretary Sullivan as they related to NASA. The two piloted the Space Shuttle *Challenger* on its mission into space in 1984. Together with Sally Ride, the three worked closely together during the investigation of the *Challenger* and *Columbia* space shuttle disasters.

Today, Secretary Sullivan called on her old friend to perform another important function, one that was *short on ceremony, and long on disaster.* He was going to brief the White House staff and the National Security Council on the threat of AR3222.

Lemmon passed through the southwest gate of the White House complex and presented the guard with his NOAA-issued identification card. The guard quickly found his name on the appointment list, and Lemmon was escorted up West Executive Avenue toward the West Basement entrance.

Once there, his identification was checked again, and another secret service agent delivered him down the stairs, past the White House Mess, which was being cleaned up following morning breakfast for senior White House staff.

They approached a locked door and Lemmon was provided access for his first, and last, visit to the brain center of the White House. Behind these layers of security was the White House Situation

Room—a five-thousand-square-foot complex of rooms located on the ground floor of the West Wing. The main conference room was surrounded on three sides by two small offices, multiple workstations, computers, and sophisticated communications equipment.

The well-appointed space was soundproofed, but small and slightly cramped. Every square foot was functional. Most visitors were impressed by the location and technology but were often surprised at the compact size.

While it was widely known that important meetings were held here, the importance of the Situation Room in the daily activities of the National Security Council and White House staff, together with its critical role in Washington's network of key national security operations and intelligence centers, was less understood.

It was commonly referred to as *The Woodshed*. The Situation Room was born out of frustration on the part of President John Kennedy after the Bay of Pigs debacle in Cuba. President Kennedy felt betrayed by the conflicting advice and information coming to him from the various agencies that comprised the nation's defense departments. Kennedy ordered the bowling alley built during the Truman presidency removed and replaced with the Situation Room. It was his way of gathering all the players in one room so they couldn't point fingers of blame in other directions.

Before the age of electronics, President Kennedy required at least one Central Intelligence analyst to remain in the Situation Room at all times. The analyst would work a twenty-hour shift and sleep on a cot during the night.

Other Presidents, like Nixon and Ford, never used the Situation Room. In most cases, a visit from the President was a formal undertaking, happening only on rare occasions. President George H.W. Bush, a former CIA head, would frequently call the Situation Room and ask if he could stop by and say hello.

Lemmon didn't expect to see the President this morning, but he certainly expected his briefing to make its way upstairs rather quickly. He took his seat at the opposite end table from several empty chairs which were reserved for the White House Chief of Staff, the National Security Advisor, and the President's Chief Political Advisor. He was greeted with a few smiles, but was largely ignored by the other attendees, who knew each other from their daily activities.

Everyone at the table except him was provided the day's briefing reports called the Morning Book. A compilation of the State Department's Morning Summary, the National Intelligence Daily and other agency-specific advisories, the Morning Book set the tone for the business of the White House on any given day.

The first order of business was AR3222 and Lemmon's presentation of a threat analysis to the highest levels of government. Lemmon was warned that the White House Chief of Staff was gruff and abrasive. He was not interested in long explanations. Further, Lemmon was told the President ran her administration on polling data, focus group interaction, and the advice of her political team. The media portrayed the President as being deliberate and thoughtful in her decision-making. In reality, she made decisions based on public perception and political impact.

"Good morning, all," announced the Chief of Staff as he entered the room and quickly took his seat. As expected, he was followed by the head of the NSA and the Chief Political Advisor. Lastly, to the apparent surprise of most in the room, the Secretary of Homeland Security walked in as the door closed behind him. A few heads darted around, looking for an empty chair, but there were none. "Secretary Blumenthal will be joining us for a moment."

"I'll stand, thank you," said Blumenthal. "I won't be here long."

The Chief of Staff continued. "Ordinarily, we would discuss the President's schedule first and then focus on matters in the Morning book, but today we have a special guest with us who only carries an L-Clearance." Lemmon's L-Clearance was hastily issued through the Department of Energy to allow him access to classified information up to and including Secret data and special L-Clearance limited information. The Situation Room regulars all held Top Secret Department of Defense clearance levels.

General Mark Welsh, Chief of Staff of the Air Force, was in

attendance and spoke up to introduce Lemmon. "Many of you may recognize today's liaison from NOAA, David Lemmon. He's a retired major from our Air Force and successfully piloted several Space Shuttle missions. Thank you for joining us today, Major." General Welsh sat down and motioned for Lemmon to take the floor.

Lemmon stood in awe of the entire situation. As he approached retirement, he had performed many tasks for his country, but none was more important than this one. His job was to inform the leaders of the greatest nation on the planet, not to convince them to take action. However, based upon the data, the United States, and possibly much of the planet, was at risk, so he didn't plan to sugarcoat it.

"Thank you, General Welsh," he started. "I'll get right to the point because time is of the essence. We are facing a catastrophic solar event the likes of which this nation has never experienced. Within fifteen hours, the entire United States, and most of the world, may be thrust into a world without power."

The room erupted in conversation. Pages were flipped through the Morning Book, searching for the source of this proclamation. Others looked to General Welsh for affirmation that Lemmon wasn't insane. But through the brief series of outbursts, Secretary Blumenthal and the President's chief advisors remained stoic. *They know.*

"Please, everyone, settle down," said the Chief of Staff. "Major Lemmon, please continue."

"Thank you, sir," started Lemmon. "With your staff's assistance, may I pull the image up on the screens?"

"Of course." An aide approached Lemmon, and he gave her instructions on the selected imagery to be revealed from his MacBook. The first photo appeared.

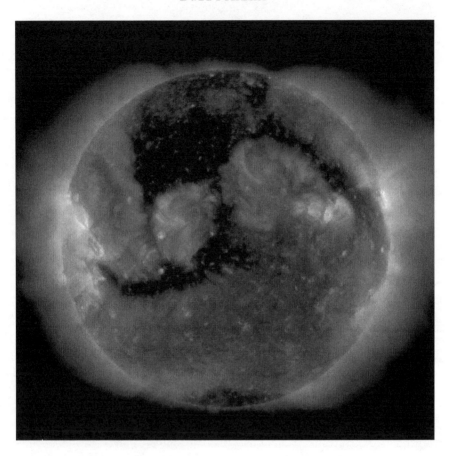

One of the attendees muttered the word *incredible*.

"Approximately four hours ago, a coronal hole, which has been monitored by facilities around the world, released an Earth-directed solar flare," continued Lemmon. He pointed to a large dark space on the upper half of the sun. "This void on the solar disk, identified as Active Region 3222, is the largest of its kind on record. Encompassing nearly half of the visible surface of the Sun, it had remained dormant for two days, until just after oh-four-hundred hours."

"Major, how is this solar flare different from others that we experience on a daily basis?" asked General Welsh.

"Sir, a relatively benign X3.3 flare has already hit the planet and is being absorbed by our magnetosphere in the ordinary course. There have been the usual reports of radio disruptions and flight navigational anomalies. However, the Space Weather Prediction Center is anticipating a coronal mass ejection to follow, which will carry the power of an X58 solar event. This could happen at any time, although forecasters point to later tonight."

Once again, the seated members in the Situation Room began to talk loudly amongst themselves. Only Blumenthal and the Chief of Staff remained calm.

Blumenthal spoke first. "How accurate are these forecasts?"

"Confirmed and reconfirmed, Mr. Secretary," replied Lemmon. "The X58 solar flare is unprecedented. The bigger impact will be felt when we are hit with the accompanying coronal mass ejection. We believe it to be larger than the infamous Carrington Event of 1859. As the CME makes its way towards Earth, it will gather particles and accelerate with the solar winds. We've never experienced anything like it."

Lemmon leaned over to the aide and asked her to bring up another image. He moved to the side so the participants could see the entire rendering. He continued.

"Because the CME is slower moving, we can more accurately predict the window of impact. This is the computer model of the CME and the accompanying solar wind colliding with Earth's atmosphere at twenty-three hundred hours."

"A direct hit?" asked one of the attendees.

"My god!" exclaimed another.

Lemmon continued. "The impact of the CME will generate huge electrical currents in Earth's upper atmosphere. More likely than not, the areas closest to the poles will be hit with large currents that will be transferred into electrical substations and disbursed throughout the power grid. It will have the impact of several nuclear electromagnetic bombs detonated over America simultaneously."

"An EMP?"

"Yes, General."

"Have you been able to measure the strength of the CME?" asked the Chief of Staff.

"We have, sir," replied Lemmon. "For the technical aspects and potential effects of the impact for this solar event, I need to defer to Dr. Andrea Stanford of the Atacama Large Millimeter Array, or ALMA, located in northern Chile." Once again, Lemmon instructed the aide to manipulate the screens in the Situation Room. Dr. Stanford appeared on three of them, although the static reception made it difficult to see her.

"Hello," said Dr. Stanford, whose audio was working fine, but the video was experiencing interference.

"Dr. Stanford, thank you for joining us," said Lemmon. "Due to the interference we're experiencing on this end, we'll dispense with the preliminaries. The first question for you is whether you have been able to measure the strength of the inbound coronal mass ejection?"

"Yes, sir," replied Dr. Stanford. "The CME will generate a geomagnetic storm, which is measured in disturbance storm time, or Dst. In layman's terms, this describes how hard a CME shakes up Earth's magnetic field. A typical Dst will be equal to negative fifty on the nanotesla scale. As you can tell by this transmission, the earth is experiencing the effects of a negative fifty influence at this time. Several decades ago, the worst geomagnetic storm ever recorded caused power outages across Quebec, Canada. The 1989 event registered a negative six hundred on the nanotesla scale."

Lemmon moved toward the microphone and directed a question

to Dr. Stanford. "I realize we didn't have sophisticated instruments in the nineteenth century, but are you able to provide us an estimate of the strength of the Carrington Event? Most of us know the effect on the nation's limited telegraph system."

"Yes," started Dr. Stanford. "Several modern studies estimate the strength of the September 1859 geomagnetic storm to be in the range of negative eight hundred to negative seventeen hundred. That's triple the 1989 storm."

"Dr. Stanford, this is Secretary Blumenthal of the Department of Homeland Security," he said as he approached the front of the room. "Do you have an opinion as to the effect a Carrington-level event would have on our power grid today?"

"I do," replied Dr. Stanford. "David, would you mind showing them the image of the at-risk transformer capacity, designated by state?"

"Okay." Lemmon provided the proper image to the aide.

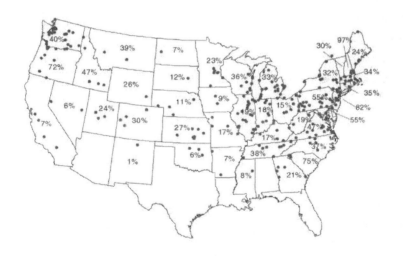

"Go ahead, Dr. Stanford, the image is onscreen," said Lemmon.

"What you are viewing is a map showing the at-risk transformer capacity for a negative seventeen hundred nanotesla geomagnetic field disturbance based upon the data for the Carrington Event. Regions with high percentages of at-risk capacities, such as in the northeast, could experience long-duration outages extending for several years. Lower percentages, as indicated in the regions like the southwest, would experience shorter outages, assuming the interconnected power grid doesn't completely overwhelm those transformers via a cascading collapse."

Lemmon turned to the people who would advise the President on what action to take. He needed to sum it up for them.

"It's hard to overstate just how much this solar event will shock our lives. Of course, the power will go out as depicted in the map, as would the Internet and most of the nation's critical infrastructure. In places with electronically controlled water supplies, toilets and sewage treatment systems would stop working, creating a disastrous public health problem. Perishable food and medication would be lost. Banks and financial markets would not function. Gas pumps would go offline. The list is long."

Blumenthal walked back to the head of the room and whispered to the Chief of Staff and the President's political advisor. He was about to exit the room when Dr. Stanford spoke again.

"Excuse me a moment, but I need to be clear about something."

Blumenthal stopped and walked a few steps toward the screen.

"Go ahead, Doctor," he said.

"The image I've provided was merely a hypothetical model for the Carrington Event based upon negative seventeen hundred nanoteslas. That is not the theoretical model for the AR3222 solar event headed towards Earth."

"How does it differ?" asked Lemmon.

"Our predictions for this event are in the range of six thousand to eight thousand negative nanoteslas."

"What does that mean in terms of the effect on the power grid?"

"Blackout. Total blackout."

# CHAPTER 15

**15 Hours**
**8:25 a.m., September 8**
**Davidson Academy**
**Nashville, Tennessee**

"I hope you won't be late, Alex," said Madison as she exited Interstate 24 onto Old Hickory Boulevard. "I can't believe the traffic today. There weren't any accidents, just cars and trucks in every direction."

Alex was oblivious to her mom as she scrolled through the news sites online, seeking the latest update on the potential for auroras, a solar flare, or anything space weather related. CNN provided one news story which regurgitated the UK *Daily Mail* report. She scrolled through Twitter, searching the hashtag *#AR3222* and *#solarflare*. Most of the tweets involved pictures of the northern lights in Europe. Dr. Stanford's Twitter account promised a video update at one o'clock. She'd try to watch the YouTube upload before her Spanish I class.

Despite being chastised several times by her Mom, Alex continually bounced through the various satellite news stations, to no avail. The Fox & Friends crew brought a live report about the northern lights from its affiliate in Presque Isle, Maine, near the Canadian border. After some playful banter with the reporter about the Carrington Event, Steve Doocy issued a stern warning to *all of you telegraph operators out there to be mindful of the phone lines getting burned up today.*

Alex didn't find their jokes or lack of professionalism amusing. Nor did Alex laugh as her mom pulled into the drop off lane and she saw several senior guys were walking toward school, fashioning tinfoil hats. *Nobody was taking this seriously.*

*Or were they?*

"Mom, doesn't the parking lot look empty to you?" she asked.

Madison glanced around and then replied, "It does. Maybe some kids took off this week for a vacation around Labor Day."

Alex just shook her head. "If that were the case, why wasn't it empty like this yesterday?" she asked sarcastically.

"Listen, Alexis, I don't know the answer to that. I know how you feel about this solar flare and it's easy to look around for signs to support your thoughts on the subject."

"Fine," she replied and hastily tried to open the door before the truck was stopped. Alex knew something was coming. She could sense it, and not just because it was the topic of conversation in Mr. Stark's class. She had a strong feeling something was about to happen. *Something unpleasant—like a premonition.*

Before Alex opened the door, she turned to her mother. "Mom, I have to turn my phone off while in school. Will you promise to keep the news on? Promise me that you'll install the solar flare app we talked about yesterday. Please?"

Madison reached for her and they hugged. Maybe she was a little too overanxious. Alex wasn't paranoid, just hyperaware. She needed her mom to believe in her.

"I promise, Alex," said Madison, looking into Alex's eyes. "I have some errands to run today. I'll keep monitoring news reports, and I will install that FlareAware app as soon as you're inside."

"You remembered the name?" asked Alex, who was trying not to become an emotional *twit*.

"Yes, honey, of course I did. Moms do listen, you know."

"Not always." Alex started to laugh and wiped a tear from her cheek. She felt better.

"That's true; guilty as charged. But this time, *I am listening*, and I want you to know that you can always count on your daddy and me, okay?"

"Okay. I love you, Mom." Alex hugged her mom and scooted out of the truck, grabbing her backpack from the rear seat as she went. She bounded up the sidewalk toward the double door entry. She gave her mom one last smile and then turned her phone back on and set it to vibrate. *Just in case.*

# CHAPTER 16

**12 Hours**
**11:20 a.m., September 8**
**Dallas Cowboys Training Facilities**
**Ford Center at The Star**
**Frisco, Texas**

Jerry Jones spared no expense when it came to his beloved Dallas Cowboys franchise. But the axiom *it takes money to make money* clearly applied in his approach to business. Football was a game for the fans, but it was big business to the NFL and its owners.

When the Cowboys' latest revolutionary project opened in Frisco, located north of Dallas, the move was hailed as shifting the model for NFL training facilities from a place to hang your cleats and shoulder pads to a complete fan experience.

Not only was The Star the home of the Cowboys' offices, but it included two outdoor practice fields, a twelve-thousand-seat indoor stadium, a retail shopping venue, and a sixteen-story Omni hotel and convention center.

Then there was the exclusive Cowboys Club, where today's meeting and follow-up luncheon was being held. Jones was the consummate entertainer, and the opportunity to showcase his new high end dining facility overlooking the field was too good to pass up.

Colton's mind wandered as the Super Bowl Halftime negotiations continued between his legal team and negotiators for the NFL. He felt guilty for dismissing Alex's concerns over this solar flare situation. While the day-to-day burden of raising their daughter rested on Madison's shoulders, Colton strived to be a good father who showed not only love for his only child but to also be the type of parent who really *listened* to his kid.

He recognized that times had changed in the twenty-some years since he went through his teens. All of the pressures and dangers facing teens twenty years ago were happening at an even younger age. The temptations of sex, gambling, drinking, and drugs were more prevalent than in his youth. The media and pop culture seemed to celebrate these things rather than discourage them. While he and Madison understood they couldn't raise their daughter in a bubble, they could certainly be there to help manage the stresses and pressures of Alex's life.

Communication was the key. Colton might remember what it was like to be a teenager back in the day, but Alex knew what it was like to be a teenager *today*. As parents, he and Madison discovered that not only could they learn a few things from their teenage daughter as she raced toward adulthood, but admired Alex's willingness to prove her maturity and readiness to take on responsibilities.

Alex was trying to show her parents that maturity by, in a level-headed manner, doing the research and presenting a plausible scenario to them regarding a potential solar flare. Colton failed his daughter last night, and he hoped he didn't break her spirit. Colton felt guilty, and he was looking for an opportunity to reach out to Alex.

The deep voice of the oldest of the NFL negotiators brought Colton back to the present. "In the fifty-plus years of the NFL's presentation of the Super Bowl, the halftime show has become synonymous with the biggest names in entertainment. Hundreds of millions of people around the world will be introduced to your client. Our request is not unreasonable."

The exchange wasn't heated, but clearly a member of Colton's legal team was aggravated. "I don't disagree with the magnitude of this event, but what you're asking is out of the norm. What do you think, Colton?"

"Um, I'm sorry. I was making a few notes."

"Colton, they're asking the talent to contribute to the expenses of the event."

The request caught Colton by surprise, and he immediately got his head back in the game. "What kind of contribution?"

"Each year, the costs of production for the halftime event increase substantially. This year will be no exception. Between the extraordinary security on the field and the significant costs associated with the lighting, it should come as no surprise that additional funds will be needed from the performers to defray these expenses."

It was time for Colton to close this deal. He sat up in his chair and stared down the NFL negotiating team. "Gentlemen, this is where I draw the line in the sand. My client doesn't want an asterisk by his name for being the only artist to *pay to play* in the Super Bowl. He wants to proudly announce that he will accompany his peers in a fantastic halftime performance based upon his talents and merit and not the size of his bank account."

Colton's granddaddy taught him not to hem-haw around. *Get to the point, boy*, his granddaddy would say. During any negotiation, it was always appropriate to be respectful and especially listen to the other side's questions. Their questions were an insight into their minds. You also had to negotiate with some wiggle room.

*Pay to play? Not gonna happen*—and it didn't.

The group took a break for lunch, and Colton excused himself to hit the restroom. His real reason for breaking away was to send a text to Madison. He expressed his feelings about shutting Alex down last night, and Madison agreed. They also discussed whether the threat was real. While they both agreed the government and the news stations would advise of any impending disaster, there was no harm in getting prepared.

C: Think of it this way. People buy insurance against losses from hurricanes, floods, and tornadoes.

M: Can you buy solar flare insurance?

C: Very funny. Pick up some extra batteries, food, and water. Basics.

M: I could buy a couple extra of everything.

C: Yeah. Stock up.

M: I've got this. Go back and play with your Cowboys.

C: After lunch, we're touring the Cowboys Cheerleaders studio and practice center.

M: What? No.

C: Yup. Gotta run. Love you!

M: Come back here, mister!

# CHAPTER 17

**12 Hours**
**11:50 a.m., September 8**
**Broadway Avenue**
**Nashville, Tennessee**

Before Madison left the house, she conducted a little online research. All she knew about prepping was getting ready for a big Thanksgiving meal or making arrangements for a get-together. Naturally, Madison was curious about what kind of person called themselves a prepper. She thought of the people at the bookstore yesterday. They looked like ordinary people, although wearing clashing styles of camo clothing should be considered a fashion faux pas. Other than that, they were just like them.

So what made them tick? Why would somebody choose to become a prepper? Madison decided to search prepper mentality, and here came the results.

Prepper mental illness
Prepper mentally defective
Prepper declared mentally defective

Was this what people thought about preppers? Madison learned years ago that the news and entertainment media could not be trusted. They deliberately slanted their particular means of mass communication toward a decidedly liberal agenda. She also suspected that Google tilted their web and news search results in a similar fashion. But an obscure search term like this yielded results that were most often what the Google user was seeking. *Most people think preppers are deranged!*

Madison taught Alex how to avoid succumbing to peer pressure. The easiest way was to say *NO* like you meant it. How did preppers overcome the peer pressure of being labeled *mentally defective?* They must be a resilient bunch to prevent public perception from swaying them from what seemed like a reasonable goal—preparedness.

Colton needed her to pick up a few things so she headed into Nashville. So many concepts were consuming Madison's thoughts. She continued up Broadway across the interstate overpass, thinking about the concept of prepping. Unless you had unlimited resources or a crystal ball, it would be impossible to prepare for every contingency—especially those that hadn't happened in a hundred years or more. Yet they'd happened. The world had experienced many catastrophic events, including massive solar flares, deadly pandemics, and volcanic eruptions. The nation's economy was in shambles and arguably on the brink of collapse. Madison remembered what happened to the Roman Empire from her studies in college.

Then there was their society. This was a regular topic of the sermons on Sunday at their church. Madison understood avoiding sin and temptation were a part of Bible teachings since the beginning. In reality, it was also a battle between right and wrong.

Something considered wrong a hundred years ago was not only accepted now, but encouraged. Exhibit A was premarital sex. Madison knew times had changed. But why? Why was out-of-wedlock sex not only accepted, but encouraged?

As Madison became stuck in traffic in front of her church at the corner of Seventh and Broadway, she realized she was so deep in thought that she forgot to turn back at Tenth Avenue to stop by Colton's office and pick up the files he requested.

She stared at the two-hundred-year-old church where she and Colton were married. She didn't always believe in God. As a child, she went to First Baptist with her family because she had to. As she grew older, she started to *see*. There was that seminal moment when she accepted Christ into her life and never doubted her faith again.

At this moment, she had a similar revelation. It started with Colton's text about insurance. He wrote that *people buy insurance against losses from hurricanes, floods, and tornadoes.* Prepping was like insurance, except not in the normal sense. It was insurance against catastrophic events that you hoped would never occur. If they happened, you could be ready, or at least more ready than others. If you prepped for the worst and nothing happened, you hadn't lost anything. At least you had the peace of mind to know you could survive a catastrophe, in whatever form it took.

She circled the block and headed back toward West End, completely abandoning what brought her downtown in the first place. Her mind was racing now. It was almost euphoric.

From what she read, preppers strongly believed in self-reliance. They equated self-reliance with freedom. All it took was a little self-discipline, sacrifice, and planning to lead a self-reliant lifestyle. *There's nothing wrong with that. Who cares what other people's perceptions are?*

Without realizing it, she was racing towards Barnes & Noble to buy that EMP book the preppers were waiting for yesterday. She pushed her way through traffic, slapping the ceiling as she crossed under two yellow lights when they turned red—*kissing the ceiling*, as she and Colton always called it.

Like most aspects of a person's life, it came down to making choices. First, she had to get her head in the right place and commit to taking care of her family. Second, she had to make some decisions. She had absolutely no clue where to begin. The bookstore would be the first stop. *Then what? Where the heck do I start?*

Her phone buzzed. It was a text message from Colton.

# CHAPTER 18

**11 Hours**
**12:22 p.m., September 8**
**West End Avenue**
**Nashville, Tennessee**

Madison read the text from her husband. It was succinct—*Don't panic. Get extra of everything. Love you!* One thing the Rymans didn't do was panic. When she experienced complications with the birth of Alex, they didn't panic. When she and Colton were told Madison couldn't have any more children as a result, they were devastated, but they didn't panic. When she quit her job and money was tight, they didn't panic. After they'd just purchased their new home in Belle Meade and Colton lost his highest-producing client to a tragic car accident, they didn't panic.

They persevered.

Every family experienced loss in some form. Those who fought through the complications, whether self-inflicted or unexpected, could come out on the other side a better person if that was their character. Those individuals who lived their life seeking pity for their troubles might not have the gravitas it took to survive a catastrophic event.

Madison knew the Rymans were tough. She was thrilled that her husband was thinking along the same lines as she was—*get ready*.

When she left the house, she was still unsure if this was the right thing to do. After Colton's text, she was convinced. Her first stop was Barnes & Noble, where she sought the assistance of a store clerk to find the book from yesterday's signing. That was easy. Then she asked a question that sent the young man's brain into circuit overload.

"Do you have any books on prepping?"

He looked at her like a deer in headlights. No answer.

"You know, preparedness. Preppers? Anything?"

He thought for a moment and then replied, "I can show you the books about camping and hiking." As he led her towards the rear of the store, Madison observed the other shoppers. They were sipping on their limited-time Starbucks Fizzio sodas that were still available because it was hot as Hades outside. "Here you are, ma'am. You'll also find fitness, diet and health, and medical books here as well."

"Thank you," said Madison as she grabbed a copy of a book called *The Survival Wilderness Handbook* off the shelf. She spied another book called *The Prepper's Cookbook. That's two.*

Then she recalled what the author said yesterday to the people standing in line. Beans, Band-Aids, and bullets, plus shelter. Here was another one for the stack—*Ultimate Survival Manual* by *Outdoor Life*. She thumbed through the table of contents. These three survival guides, plus the EMP book, which contained an extensive prepper's checklist, would do for starters.

Madison checked out and then thought about her priorities. Books were great resources, but there might not be enough time to read them. She thumbed through the prepper's checklist. Their food pantry was pretty well stocked with at least a week's worth of meals.

She glanced at her watch and realized she had plenty of time to make another stop. But where? Her mind raced as the adrenaline kicked into full gear. Dick's Sporting Goods on Charlotte Pike was the closest store she could think of. Target was over there too.

After making her purchase, she took the neighborhood streets, avoiding the congestion of White Bridge Road, and found her way to Charlotte Pike. Traffic wasn't bad, but the parking lot around Target and Dick's was very full.

She hustled past the monument in the shape of a guitar, which was placed in front of Best Buy in honor of the now deceased legendary country music star George Jones. Two pickup trucks were parked in front of the store, loading canoes and camping supplies. The outside of the store was hectic, but the inside of the sporting goods store was worse.

Every checkout counter had a lengthy line. Madison made her way past a congregation of people in the front of the store who were waiting for their friends and family to pay for their things. Several areas of the store like the Team Shop and Alex's beloved Golf Shop were devoid of customers. Other parts, especially the gun counter and camping supplies, were packed.

The gun counter was her first stop. She was the only woman in line waiting for a lone clerk. While she waited, she studied the checklist in the book she purchased at Barnes & Noble. The last dozen pages covered everything from food to weapons to medical supplies. She made mental notes regarding the items on the list. Finally, after twenty minutes, she was able to speak with a second clerk who arrived to assist.

"How may I help you?" he asked.

That was when it dawned on her. She had no idea what to buy. "Well, um, I don't know." She hesitated until she heard the groans of the impatient men behind her.

"Okay," the clerk started. "Maybe I can help. What do you want the gun for?"

Madison's mind immediately thought of hunting, but then reality set in. *There aren't many deer and antelope in Belle Meade. Where would we hunt?* Protection. *We need it for protection and security.*

"Protection," she blurted out. "I guess the most important thing for us is security."

"Okay, now we're getting somewhere," said the clerk. "By far the best all-around weapon for security, and hunting, is the versatile shotgun. He reached behind the counter and showed her a black and brushed metallic shotgun. "For home defense, this weapon is very forgiving for nervous aiming. You don't have to be particularly accurate to do some damage against an intruder."

He racked the slide up and down, creating a loud, metallic CRACK CRACK. Madison jumped back slightly before regaining her composure. The men behind her snickered.

"It's also perfectly suited for hunting small game, and larger animals if you have the right shells."

Madison thought for a moment and then remembered her father-in-law's shotgun that Colton put in the garage somewhere. She could use that one.

"I think we have a shotgun already," she said. "What are the other options?"

"Get her an AR-15," said one of the men behind her.

"Better yet, an AR-10," added another sarcastically. "Then she can be a real bad …"

The salesclerk was a nice young guy and seemed genuinely interested in helping Madison. He continued with her options.

"Ma'am, we're sold out of the guns they mentioned, and if you aren't experienced, they might not be for you anyway. Let me suggest a handgun, namely this nine millimeter made by Beretta. It's the official sidearm of our military and is very dependable. For your smaller hands and for concealed-carry purpose, this Series 92 Compact is a great choice. This one comes in all black; it's less flashy."

He handed her the gun and she took it from him with apprehension. She had never held a real handgun before. At first, she was a little afraid. The weight felt good and she gripped it. She could easily get three fingers on the grip for control. She liked it.

"Okay," she choked out. Then she thought for a moment. *Alex, too?* She set the weapon back on the counter. "I mean okay. I'll take it. In fact, give me three of them. Bullets too."

"Yeah, I wish," said the heavyset man behind her who was, frankly, starting to make Madison mad with his attitude.

"Ma'am, I'm sorry, but you can only purchase one at a time. The President passed an executive order after she was inaugurated that prohibited multiple sales of two or more guns to the same purchaser within five business days."

"Oh, okay. I didn't realize," she started. She reached for the gun and asked, "Do I pay you or up front on the way out."

This caused an uproar of laughter behind her. Madison had never contemplated buying a gun, so she was completely unaware of the procedure. She thought that showing the checkout clerk her driver's license and social security card would be sufficient. People voted and received government welfare with less identification.

"Ma'am, you'll need to fill out this Form 4473 required by the Bureau of Alcohol, Tobacco, Firearms, and Explosives. We'll submit the form on your behalf, and you should be able to pick up your weapon in five to seven business days."

"When?" she asked.

"Five to seven business days, ma'am," the clerk responded. "There is a tremendous backlog in background checks, at both the state and federal level."

Madison got frustrated. She didn't need a gun in five to seven business days. She needed it now. If nothing happened by tomorrow, then she probably wouldn't need one at all.

"Don't you have any guns I can buy today?"

"No, ma'am," he replied. "Everything requires a background check."

She looked at the salesclerk in disbelief and walked away.

She gathered herself and sought out the stacks of ammunition on tables near the gun counter. The inventory levels were dwindling. She found the shotgun shells and was dumbfounded. She had no idea which ones would work in their shotgun, so she purchased a variety and decided to let Colton figure it out.

After picking up a dozen boxes of slugs and buckshot, she filled her cart with some compact nutrition bars called MRE food rations, which contained three thousand six hundred calories each. She purchased a medical kit, some camping gear, and then she came across a device called a LifeStraw.

She thought about the ramifications of a major power outage. Would Nashville's Metro Water Service be able to distribute water without power? It was so easy to get dehydrated. Her sparkling pool came to mind. The pump and filter system wouldn't work, but the water could be purified. The LifeStraw packaging claimed to remove virtually all bacteria, and it surpassed standards for water filters. She could filter two hundred and fifty gallons with each device. She couldn't calculate how long that would last them, but she hoped three would do the trick.

Finally, while she waited in line, she thought about her favorite television show on CBS—*Survivor*. Making fire was always a challenge. She saw some emergency fire starter flints on an end cap of the register. She grabbed the last four of them.

Madison was on her way to being a prepper.

# CHAPTER 19

**11 Hours**
**12:38 p.m., September 8**
**Dallas Cowboys Training Facilities**
**Ford Center at The Star**
**Frisco, Texas**

One of his attorneys leaned over and whispered to Colton, "Have you heard about this solar flare thing? I guess a lot of flights are being rerouted, and now they're talking about potential power outages."

"Where did you hear that?" Colton whispered back. "Is it something official—out of Washington?"

"Nah, just news reports," he replied. "But you know how they can get. When there isn't some political scandal to talk about, they grab onto any kind of drama to boost ratings."

Colton thought for a moment and then pulled his iPhone out of his jacket pocket. He finished the glass of water he had been nursing. He decided to look online for himself.

The first stop was FoxNews.com, but it yielded nothing. There was a brief mention in a video article about the potential for northern lights into the American Heartland, but no details. Then he went to his bookmark for the Drudge Report.

Jerry Jones paraded out Dez Bryant, Tony Romo, and former University of Tennessee star Jason Witten to meet the contingent as lunch concluded. Colton wanted to meet Witten, who had become one of the top tight ends in the NFL, but he was intent on finding an update. Drudge had a tendency to sensationalize his headlines to grab attention, so it was necessary to read the actual article he aggregated. One headline read *The Heat is ON*. Another simply read *ANGRY!*

He clicked on the second article and navigated his finger across the iPhone's screen to CBSNews.com, which read *Newest Hole in the Sun is a Doozy*. It was updated eleven minutes ago and contained the latest imagery from NASA.

Colton glanced through the article, oblivious to his surroundings. *New—and massive—coronal hole has developed on the sun's surface, NASA announced today. This coronal hole will be responsible for high-speed solar winds coupled with solar particles, which are expected to collide with Earth sometime Thursday evening. Potentially ruinous effects on orbiting satellites and geo-positioning systems are likely. Travelers are urged to take caution and be aware that flights are being rerouted or canceled altogether per the FAA.*

It was the last paragraph of the article that struck Colton. *Why do the news media feel it's necessary to downplay potential threats to our safety? Do they not think we can handle the truth?* The paragraph read *but the solar winds aren't all bad. They're also responsible for the beautiful auroras that will grace our skies this evening at latitudes as low as Oklahoma and Tennessee.*

Tennessee! *That's it. Am I overreacting? Something is screaming—GET READY!*

He was furiously texting Madison now. It was simple, and Colton doubted she would push back at his suggestion.

C: 911! Pull Alex out of school now! Get extra food. Be careful.

# CHAPTER 20

**10 Hours**
**1:00 p.m., September 8**
**Oval Office, The White House**
**Washington, DC**

The President stood behind her desk and stared out onto the south lawn of the White House complex. There were no activities today, and she had planned an afternoon with her daughter and two grandchildren. Her husband was fund-raising on Long Island, which gave her the opportunity to unwind. She was having difficulty separating his former presidency from hers.

Despite the earlier briefing, she didn't find a need to alter her schedule. But her Chief of Staff sent her an urgent message, so she made her way to the Oval Office to meet with key members of her national security team.

"Madame President, I apologize for interrupting your afternoon, but an update has been received from NOAA and NASA that requires your attention."

"Fine, go ahead," she bristled. "I've planned this day with my grandchildren and daughter for weeks. This better be important."

"It is, Madame President," he started.

She quickly turned around and sat in her chair. She motioned for the rest of the national security team to take seats as well. Her Chief of Staff handed her the updated report, and she glanced through it.

"These are the updated projections of a coronal mass ejection emitted from Active Region 3222 at approximately zero four hundred. Based on satellite analysis, an accurate prediction analysis has been created."

"Plain English, please," she said. "What exactly are we facing here?" She tossed the report on her desk and leaned back in her chair, clasping her fingers together across her stomach.

Secretary Sullivan replied, "In the next ten hours, the northern hemisphere of our planet will absorb the full brunt of an X58 solar flare with an accompanying coronal mass ejection greater than any in recorded history. There is a high probability our nation's critical infrastructure will be severely damaged."

"Kathryn, how is this information different from this morning's NSA briefing?" she asked.

"Madame President, the timing of these events determines the impact on Earth. As of eight this morning, we were able to provide a fairly accurate analysis of the strength of the incoming solar ejection. Now, with an additional four hours of data, we can predict the probable sphere of impact."

"Don't leave me hanging here," said the President, growing impatient.

Secretary Sullivan continued. "Based on Earth's relative positioning and our proximity to the fall equinox, we are predicting a direct hit to the northern hemisphere around twenty-three hundred hours."

The President remained silent for a moment. She spun in her chair and glanced out into the Rose Garden. "Do we have a protocol for this?"

"We do, Madame President," replied Secretary Blumenthal. "The Space Weather Preparedness Strategy, or SWPS, was adopted by the prior administration in late 2015 to prepare, respond to, and recover from potentially devastating space weather events."

"That's admirable," she interrupted. "What do the guidelines suggest?"

"The first step establishes the magnitude of the space weather event, and then we craft a response at the federal, state, and local level. Protection efforts would include assuring continuity of government, minimizing risks to our critical national infrastructure, and managing societal reaction to the event's aftermath."

"Well, at this point, I hardly see a need to implement martial law." She laughed in her own unique way. "I think it's important to figure out how we notify appropriate agencies without causing widespread panic. We do have to do everything we can, however."

"Madame President, if I may," interjected her Chief Political Advisor. "There is an action plan in place per the SWPS. Whether the next ten hours is sufficient time to implement it is not for me to decide. At this point, the media is beginning to drive the narrative. The British print media led the way early this morning, and now the cable news outlets are parading their experts out to the televisions of millions of Americans."

"Okay, I get it," said the President. "We need to issue a statement, and I assume you have a draft copy in the works."

"I do," he replied.

"Then how do we issue a public warning without causing widespread panic?"

"This is an issue that has been raised regarding the threat of near-Earth objects, NEOs, like asteroids," replied Secretary Sullivan. "A key issue associated with the hazard from NEOs is that the length of time needed to implement a mitigation plan is affected by the accuracy of the trajectory of the NEO. In the case of a solar flare, whether a geomagnetic storm warning should be issued or not depends on the data received from our satellites. In this case, we were given nearly twenty hours' notice of the solar event, but only ten hours' notice of the probability of impact."

"In other words, if we issue the order to prepare prematurely, we could unduly cause fear to the public," said the President. "But if we wait too long, then the mitigation strategy will be for naught."

"Madame President, I've been in contact with Dr. Dennis Mileti, a professor at the University of Colorado at Boulder," said Secretary Sullivan. "He's been a consultant to the SWPC in Boulder."

"What does he think?" the President asked.

Secretary Sullivan summarized. "Dr. Mileti is of the opinion there are several myths associated with providing the general public warning of an impending disaster. The first myth is panic. He believes the fear of instilling public panic has repeatedly constrained providing an endangered public with effective warnings. It typically leads to downplaying risks, which robs the public of both the time and the motivation they need to act."

"People panic easily," interjected the Chief Political Advisor. "If we issue a warning that the world is coming to an end because the sun is having a bad day and nothing happens, we'll lose credibility. Do I need to remind everyone of the public perception hit we took after cancelling the Daytona 500?"

"We have to craft a measured response to the *experts* that are hitting the news networks," replied Secretary Sullivan. "I can call a press conference and issue a statement that exudes control and composure while providing the facts as we know them. If the media doesn't sense panic, it won't hit the airwaves to create panic. Perhaps we can invite the White House press corps to photograph and observe the President playing with her grandkids."

"Good idea," said the President. She swiveled and looked out into the beautiful, sunny day. "I'll play ball with them on the South Lawn for a photo op. You know, just another day."

"Okay, I can sign off on that," said the Chief Political Advisor, turning his attention to Secretary Sullivan. "But keep your statement terse—simple language and just a few words."

"With all due respect," started Secretary Sullivan. "I think that's a mistake. I can't tell the American people they are at risk and then not give them sufficient information to create an informed decision. They will turn to the media for answers, and that will ramp up the speculation."

The conversation was now becoming heated. The Chief Political Advisor shot back, "You can't cry wolf either. If this solar flare does nothing but cause a lot of pretty colors in the sky and you take us to the functional equivalent of DEFCON 2, the public will never respond to our warnings again. What if the Russians fire off a nuke and the public ignores our alerts?"

"Then we'll deal with that if it happens. I'm telling everyone in this room that AR3222 has delivered its own nuclear payload, and it's headed right for us. Whether our country is hit by a Russian nuke or this massive CME, the result is the same—lights out!"

# CHAPTER 21

**10 Hours**
**1:00 p.m., September 8**
**Davidson Academy**
**Nashville, Tennessee**

Madison hurried through the security checkpoint inside the entrance of Davidson Academy and started down the hallway to where she thought Alex's algebra class was located. The security guard hollered after her.

"Mrs. Ryman!" the guard shouted. "You'll need to stop by the principal's office first and state your reason for being here. Most likely, you'll be accompanied by a guidance counselor to your daughter's room."

Madison stopped and listened to the guard. But as soon as he turned to clear another visitor, she hurried down the hall. She ducked down a corridor toward her right and began to walk briskly, hoping to avoid detection. She contemplated removing her sandals, which made a loud *clap* on the polished tile floors as she moved from room to room.

She peered through the six-inch-wide, two-foot-tall windows that were located in each of the classroom doors. At the next-to-last room before the end of the hallway, she saw Alex sitting in the second row. She reached for the doorknob and then hesitated.

*Last chance, Maddie*, she whispered, referring to herself with the name only her husband was allowed to use.

She gently knocked on the door and entered, startling the teacher, who turned toward her. Alex immediately saw her and mouthed the words—*What, Mom?*

"I am so sorry to interrupt, but I need my daughter, Alexis Ryman, to come with me. We have a family situation to deal with."

The kids in the classroom started to whisper among themselves, and the teacher admonished them to settle down. He looked past Madison, apparently expecting to see a school administrator.

"Have you checked in at the front office, Mrs. Ryman?"

"Oh, yes, of course," she lied. "I told them I knew where Alex's class was located and that an escort wasn't necessary. They were all very busy and told me to have a nice day."

Madison fidgeted nervously and wiggled her hand to encourage Alex to get out of her chair to join her.

"Well, this is not the normal procedure. Just allow me to call Mrs. Grace and confirm—"

"Oh, that won't be necessary. Again, I'm sorry to interrupt. We'll just be on our way. Come on, honey." Madison pushed past him and motioned for Alex to come along. Alex gathered her things, finally, and started toward the door.

"Mom," said Alex, stopping just short of leaving, "what's wrong? If I leave school early, I won't be able to play in my match this afternoon. Can't this wait two more hours?"

"No, Alex, it can't." The teacher started to dial the front office again. "Your dad sent me for you. We have to go, *now!*"

"But, Mom," started Alex, but then they both heard her cell phone vibrate in the pocket of her school-issued blue blazer. Alex pulled out the phone and looked at the alert with her mom. She studied the display, which read *FlareAware Alert—G5 Extreme—Geomagnetic Storm Warning.*

"Let's go," said Madison and grabbed her daughter by the hand.

"Wait," came the voice of the teacher from inside the classroom, but it was too late. Madison and Alex ran through the hallways toward the front of the building, where their SUV remained parked with the hazard lights flashing.

The security guard left his post to report to the principal's office following the teacher's phone call. He and a guidance counselor chased after the Ryman women as they scurried out of the building.

"Thelma and Louise!" shouted Alex as she slid into the passenger seat. Madison laughed with her daughter as they roared out of the parking lot.

"I'm sorry for the drama, honey."

"No prob, Mom. Is Daddy okay? Is he coming home?" asked Alex nervously.

"He's fine, honey and I think he's on his way."

Alex looked around the school parking lot. "Do you think I'll get suspended?"

"Nah. Maybe detention, or you'll write sentences. Somehow, I don't think it's going to be an issue for a while."

Madison gunned the accelerator and increased her speed as she turned off Old Hickory Boulevard onto Interstate 24 toward the city. "See what you can find on the radio."

Alex bounced through several SiriusXM channels and finally settled on CNN. She then turned her attention to the FlareAware app. She read the alerts aloud.

"An Earth-directed CME at 09:23 UTC. A G5 geomagnetic storm warning has been issued. Then there's a link to a YouTube video."

Madison glanced at the phone to see for herself and almost got hit by an eighteen-wheeler that suddenly changed lanes in front of her.

"Mom!" Alex exclaimed.

"Sorry," apologized Madison.

"Maybe I should drive." Alex laughed, partly serious.

"Not gonna happen. Are you going to the video?"

"Hang on, jeez Louise."

Alex played the video as Madison exited westbound onto Briley Parkway. She was going to avoid downtown traffic, and the loop would drop her off near the grocery stores. She glanced over at the phone again.

"I don't hear anything. Can you turn it up?" asked Madison.

"Mom, you're driving me nuts. The video doesn't have sound. It just shows this black-and-white image of a blast coming from the sun, followed by a bunch of numbers. I'm looking for Dr. Stanford's YouTube channel for an update."

Madison kept driving while Alex searched for more information online. She scrolled through the Sirius channels, but found nothing on the dedicated news networks. *Why hasn't the government issued a statement? Maybe it was nothing? Did Colton panic because Alex and I were worked up into a frenzy?*

"She hasn't issued an update, and I can't find anything else online," said Alex, interrupting Madison's inner debate. "I'm checking Twitter now."

"Why Twitter?"

"News breaks faster on Twitter than anywhere else, Mom. Everybody has a cell phone with a camera. Most people have a Twitter account. The first eyewitnesses to any major news event start on Twitter."

"Really?"

"Yes, Mom. I've told you this before."

Madison shrugged and kept driving. As Alex searched for some kind of update, Madison thought about their next move. Colton's text read *Get food.* So that was the first order of business. She and Alex would head to Kroger or Publix. Probably Kroger because she liked the fuel points.

"Wow!" exclaimed Alex. "I searched hashtag 3222 and found a lot of tweets from astronomers all over the world. Here is one from SunViewer. *Very prominent sunspot 3222 is clearly visible. Massive Earth-directed plasma. Keep an eye out for aurora.*"

"That's it. Watch for pretty skies tonight?"

"I'll keep looking, but that's it so far."

Madison was puzzled. *Where are the warnings?*

# CHAPTER 22

**10 Hours**
**1:28 p.m., September 8**
**Kroger Grocery Store**
**West End Avenue**
**Nashville, Tennessee**

Madison turned right into the aging Belle Meade Plaza at the corner of White Bridge Road and West End Avenue. CVS anchored one end of the shopping center and appeared to be fairly busy. As she drove toward the southern end of the center, which contained the Kroger store, she looked at the vacant storefronts and the homeless couple digging through a trash can on the sidewalk.

It was a sign of the stagnant economic times. The nation never recovered from the recession of '08 to '09. Over one hundred million Americans were either unemployed or had given up looking for work altogether. Sixty percent of Americans were on some form of government assistance. A malaise had beset the nation for years, and it resulted in the worst class warfare in the nation's history. Tensions existed between the wealthy and the poor, between the races, and religions.

John Winthrop, a leading figure in the creation of the Massachusetts Bay Colony in the seventeenth century, once urged the colonists to create a *city upon a hill*, a phrase derived from the Sermon on the Mount. Ronald Reagan used a similar phrase—*a shining city upon a hill*. Ronald Reagan, like John Winthrop, saw America as exceptional.

Over time, the *shining city* began to lose its luster. The thin veneer of civilization that Americans relied upon to keep order was slowly evaporating. Rot and decay had gradually overcome morals and values. At one point, as members of a civilized society, you could expect your fellow citizens to act a certain way. America was on a steady decline in that respect, and it was about to get worse.

"It looks pretty busy, Mom," said Alex. "Should we try Publix instead?"

"Let's try here first. I know this store better." Madison eased her way past shoppers leaving the store. Everything appeared to be normal, as it wasn't unusual for Wednesday, senior discount day, to be busy. She finally found a space next to West End Avenue and backed into it.

Madison hurried into the store with Alex. She had a general idea of the things she wanted to buy, and the rest she would pick up based on the checklist from the book she'd bought that morning.

"Grab your own cart, Alex. We'll probably fill them both up. Follow me. We're gonna skip the produce and deli."

"Mom, what exactly are we shopping for?" asked Alex.

"Nonperishable foods, honey. We need food that we can eat without any preparation and that will give us nutrition and energy. Think of foods that require little or no cooking too."

Madison veered toward the left through the floral department until Alex grabbed her arm.

"What about granola, nuts, and dried fruits? You know, the stuff hikers and campers eat."

Madison stopped as she realized Alex was right. When she used to hike, she planned on eating a snack every hour for energy, which included complex carbohydrates like pretzels and crackers as well as nuts and dried fruits.

"You're right. Back this way." Madison wheeled the cart around and almost took out a table of purple orchids. She headed back into the produce department, past the sushi counter, and found the wall of granola and trail mix ingredients. She and Alex began filling up the plastic bags and closing them with the twist ties.

She didn't add to their cart in the meat and seafood department. They had a deep freeze in their garage, which was full of frozen chicken, meats, and seafood. If the power went out for a significant period of time, the deep freeze would only function for so long before the food would spoil. They would have to cook it first.

Madison led Alex past the organic foods section toward the canned goods. Once again, Alex stopped her.

"Mom, wait. We can use these too." Alex turned down the aisle and stopped in front of the organic energy bars. She began to fill her cart with Clif and Larabar energy bars. Madison was impressed with Alex's cool demeanor. Although the two hadn't said it aloud, they were shopping for their survival. The choices they made in that Kroger store might determine whether they lived or died.

The next aisle, which contained canned goods and dried beans, was busy. Madison observed the usual Wednesday senior shoppers who took advantage of the five percent discount offered by Kroger. But there were others. *Like us.*

As Madison approached the dried beans and rice, she noticed a woman filling her cart with bags of beans. Her toddler was gleefully kicking his legs back and forth in the shopping cart's seat.

Madison quickly joined her and began grabbing twenty-pound bags of rice off the bottom shelf. The woman made eye contact and nodded. *She's doing the same thing!* Madison debated whether to say anything, but then decided the two needed to cooperate.

She whispered to the woman, "We need the same things. How about we take turns so that we both get what we need. Deal?"

"Deal," the woman responded as she took a bag of rice. She and Madison took turns until the shelves were emptied and the bottom of Madison's cart was full of a variety of legumes and uncooked rice. After they had finished, they looked at each other and the woman began to shed a few tears. Madison became emotional as well and moved to give her a hug.

The woman whispered to Madison, "I'm scared."

"Me too," replied Madison, holding the stranger tightly. "Take care of that beautiful boy, okay?"

The woman wiped her tears and smiled at Madison. The two mothers had shared a moment, rendered support to each other with love, and then moved on to the task at hand.

As they worked their way through the aisles, more *shoppers of the pre-apocalypse* began to appear. They pushed carts full of bottled water, batteries, and packaged meals. Madison continued to concentrate on food items, including spices to make their stockpile of beans and rice more palatable and varied.

In the paper goods section, she grabbed two large packs of toilet paper and paper towels, a three-hundred-piece disposable flatware set, several boxes of garbage bags, and several packages of Ziplocs.

The cleaning supplies section was almost skipped, but Alex reminded her mom that chlorine bleach could be used to purify water and sanitize things. They also bought several bottles of Purell.

Their last stop was the area near the pharmacy, which included medications and sports nutrition supplements. The store was filling up, and Madison felt a sense of urgency. The faces in the crowd said it all. People were on edge and in a hurry.

"Alex, let's split up here. I'll focus on medical supplies. I want you to load up on vitamins and supplements, okay?"

"Like what?" asked Alex.

Madison replied as Alex began to push her cart in that direction. "Vitamins. You know, multivitamins, mineral supplements, C, D, E and B-Complex."

"Okay," shouted Alex in response.

"Hey, protein powders too," Madison yelled back. "Grab protein mixes, the big muscle builder containers."

"Got it," came the response over the top of the first aid shelves.

Madison pulled the EMP book out of her bag and thumbed to the appendix. The list titled *Survival Medicine* was long.

"My goodness," she uttered out loud. *First Aid. Infection. Dental treatments. Pain.* She quickly became overwhelmed as her eyes darted from the book to the store shelves. *Why didn't I do this years ago?*

Her cart was almost full, but she started by grabbing one of everything. Bandages, ointments, adhesive tape, and Betadine. She then worked her way through the pain relievers and cold-relief medications. She grabbed a variety. She retrieved extra Benadryl from the shelf because it could be used for bee stings and bug bites.

As Alex reappeared, she was holding up her cell phone to show Madison another alert from FlareAware. It was another geomagnetic storm warning.

"Mom, I really think we need to go."

# CHAPTER 23

**10 Hours**
**1:35 p.m., September 8**
**Dallas Cowboys Training Facilities**
**Ford Center at The Star**
**Frisco, Texas**

Colton's palms were sweaty. Despite the cold temperatures in the conference room, he was visibly sweating. He wanted out of there! Colton couldn't remember a single word mentioned by the attorneys since he read the online articles and sent Madison the text.

"Well, it appears we have the basis for a deal, and I'll have our people in New York draft a formal agreement," said one of the suits for CBS, who remained fairly quiet while the NFL and Colton's legal team hashed out the details. "I would like to remind everyone that we need to keep this under wraps until halftime of this evening's game. Commissioner Goodell, Mr. Jones, and CBS sports director Bob Fishman will be conducting a news conference to make the formal announcement. I'd like to thank everyone for their—"

Suddenly, Jerry Jones burst into the conference room. "Everybody, I need you to listen." Jones was visibly shaken. His jacket was off and tie loosened. Something was wrong. Colton immediately felt for his phone.

"I have been advised by my staff there apparently is going to be a warning issued regarding flight travel and cancellation of public events." Jones instructed one of his aides to turn on the television monitors in the room. FoxNews with its commonly used *Breaking News* graphic filled the screens.

*"Airlines are scrambling at this hour to comply with FAA restrictions just*

*handed down as we bring you breaking news from Washington. Apparently, solar activity has suddenly increased, which is disrupting the use of GPS and other satellite-dependent devices. There are now reports of increasingly long lines at airports as passengers traveling the northernmost routes of the United States and Canada are being affected. SEA-TAC and JFK have reported two security breaches as panicked passengers rushed through TSA checkpoints in an effort to reach their departing flights. Thus far, we've received no official word from the White House, but the press pool has been put on notice that a statement will be issued by Secretary Sullivan shortly. We'll have more on this story as it develops."*

Jones continued. "I've received a phone call from Commissioner Goodell, whose flight has been grounded out of New York. He is telling me that, in all likelihood, tonight's game will be—"

But Jones was interrupted by the buzzing of muted cell phones that were set to vibrate. Within thirty seconds, text messages were received and voice mails were listened to.

Many of the attendees in the conference room, except for Colton, were receiving wireless emergency alerts. Since 9/11, public safety officials had used the emergency alert system as a reliable method of delivering warnings of impending natural or man-made disasters. Governmental websites like NOAA, FEMA, and Ready.gov provided a variety of notification options.

In Colton's home state, the Tennessee Emergency Management Agency, or TEMA, created a Mobile Preparedness App for all major cell phone platforms. In addition to warnings of an impending disaster, the app provided locations of shelters, evacuation routes, and local emergency management contacts based upon your location.

At any given time, a user could visit the app and determine the state's emergency activation level. Level five was considered normal, and level one indicated a catastrophic disaster. Colton was unaware that his state had declared a level two, major disaster.

"A solar flare?" said one of the attendees.

"Possible power outages," said another.

Jones continued. "The game is likely to be canceled. Now, I live here, so this is easy for me to say. It's possible this is a false alarm, as there is not an official statement from the President or her staff. But for any of you who would feel more comfortable getting home to your families, I suggest you leave now. I have cars waiting downstairs to take each of you to your chosen destination."

Papers were being shoveled into briefcases, and the lids snapped closed before some of the executives hit the conference room door. Pleasantries were not exchanged. Handshakes with their host were sidestepped. It was every man for himself.

Colton sat stunned for a moment before he gathered his belongings. Most of the NFL and network people flew in on private jets from New York or California. They would meet up with their aircraft at the nearby executive airport in Addison. Nobody offered him a lift. Colton realized he was the only attendee that flew on a commercial airline.

As he left, he stopped to shake the hand of the NFL icon Jerry Jones. "I want to thank you, sir, for what you have done for my client and me. I hope this is not as serious as it portends to be."

"I agree, young man. May I assume you're flying back to Nashville? You're welcome to ride this out at my lake house near Tioga."

Colton smiled and declined, saying that he wanted to get home to his family. He picked up his pace and headed down the hallway toward the winding stairwell leading to the lobby. He was remarkably calm considering he rang the warning bell with Madison an hour ago.

*Madison! Doggone it. I need to call her.* He tried in vain, but all circuits were busy. Colton suspected much of America would be lighting up the cell phone lines over the next hour, attempting to spread the word of the impending flare.

*How am I gonna get through? I need to get on a plane!*

# CHAPTER 24

**10 Hours**
**1:52 p.m., September 8**
**Sam Rayburn Tollway**
**North Dallas, Texas**

The black Lincoln Town Car raced through traffic on the toll road named for former Texas Congressman Sam Rayburn, who served as the Speaker of the U.S. House of Representatives for seventeen years, the longest tenure in history. Rayburn was actually a Tennessean by birth, having been born in Roane County near the Cumberland Plateau.

Colton tried not to watch as his driver emulated a frustrated NASCAR driver who'd rather be at the Texas Motor Speedway. Instead, Colton focused his efforts on trying to get flight information online and changing his reservation. He was not having any luck. He kept receiving a *502 Bad Gateway Error Message,* which meant the servers for the websites were overloaded. He had less luck getting through on the phone. His texts appeared to be going out, but he was unsure whether they were being delivered. It was very frustrating.

The driver found his way to DFW, and Colton immediately headed to the American Airlines ticket counter. He read the departure board while he waited in line. The first available nonstop flight left at 2:25. After that, he would have to wait until 4:44.

The line wasn't moving, and Colton craned his neck to get a better view of the ticket counter. The passengers appeared frustrated as the ticket agents stared down at their computer monitors. Ten minutes had passed, and nobody had been issued a ticket. *Something is wrong.*

It was hot and stuffy in Terminal A, and the travelers began to feel the heat under their collars as well. Colton looked at his watch and saw that it was nearly 2:00 p.m. Even if a seat was available on the earlier Nashville flight, there were so many potential passengers in line that he knew that flight was realistically out of the question. He began to doubt whether he could make the 4:44, for that matter. The TSA checkpoint lines were so slow that the FAA was recommending allowing three hours to pass through security—*under normal travel conditions*. This was hardly normal.

Colton had to make a decision. He recalled that it was roughly six hundred fifty miles or so to Nashville from Dallas, and it was all interstate. He performed the calculations in his head. The only major cities that would hold him up were Little Rock and Memphis. Little Rock had a bypass, but Memphis would be a pain in the butt. *If I average eighty miles an hour, that's eight hours. Home by 10:00. Decision made.*

Colton left the line and was headed down the escalator toward Ground Transportation and the car rental companies when he heard the PA announcement followed by groans and shouts of anger. American Airlines had just announced that their outbound flights were either grounded or canceled due to lack of equipment. Because so many flights from northern airports had been canceled, there weren't any inbound planes available to meet connections. At that moment, commercial airline travel came to a virtual standstill across the nation.

Colton ran down the remaining few steps of the escalator, pushing his way past half a dozen people. He approached the Hertz counter and was pleased to find that there was no line. He stood there patiently for a moment, waiting for a rental agent, but no one arrived. He looked around for a bell or a buzzer to ring. Nothing. But then he noticed a sign upside down on the counter that read NO CARS AVAILABLE. A frustrated customer must have slammed it down in disgust.

He immediately looked around at the other counters. The counters were vacant, but there were several signs that read NO CARS AVAILABLE.

*Now what?* Colton wandered through the rental car area, rubbing his temples and looking to his cell phone for guidance. He tried to call Madison again with no luck. He hadn't received a response to his text. *What am I gonna do? I could go back to Frisco. Maybe Jerry Jones could take me to his lake house?*

Colton began walking toward the taxi stand, and he saw a small rental car counter tucked around the corner from the main rows of the national brand names. It was called Divine Auto Rental, and there was a lonely customer service agent waiting for the next traveler. Their sign read *CARS AVAILABLE*.

Just what the good Lord ordered, he laughed to himself.

# CHAPTER 25

**10 Hours**
**1:48 p.m., September 8**
**Kroger Grocery Store**
**West End Avenue**
**Nashville, Tennessee**

Just as Madison and Alex turned their overloaded carts toward the checkout aisles, the sights and sounds of cell phones coming to life filled the aisles of the Kroger store. It was not the grocery store chain's equivalent of the famous K-Mart Blue Light Special of years past. This was a special alert of another kind—*here comes the sun, and not in a nice way*.

The State of Tennessee elected to use its Amber Alert Warning system to post a notification about the geomagnetic storm. As of 2013, AMBER Alerts, which were used exclusively for the purposes of notifying the public of a serious child-abduction case, were automatically sent through the Wireless Emergency Alerts program to all cell phone users. Everyone with a WEA-enabled phone was automatically enrolled for three alerts—presidential declarations, imminent threats like terrorist acts, and AMBER alerts.

Although a national program, it was typically utilized by local law enforcement and governments. Tennessee's governor issued an imminent threat warning regarding the coronal mass ejection inbound from the sun.

Within the store, over a span of thirty seconds, the shoppers went from dead silence to a panicked mob. Many saw the alert, which began with the words *Imminent Threat Warning*, and lost sight of the message which followed.

Earlier in the year, a much-publicized *Imminent Threat Warning* was issued by newly installed Governor Charlie Crist of Florida declaring a state of emergency in the Daytona Beach area. The Daytona 500 was cancelled moments before the green flag dropped, causing a mass panic and the deaths of seventeen people. It became a major source of embarrassment to the newly inaugurated President.

"We're under attack!"

"Terrorists!"

"Are we at war?"

The shouts of fear and hysteria filled the air amidst the sounds of metal shopping carts crashing into each other. Cell phones rang and were answered. Others attempted to reach loved ones. Madison kept her head and urged Alex to hurry to the checkout aisle.

Out of twelve available lanes, only one "twenty items or less" was open, the self-checkout, and five regular lanes. Madison resisted the urge to use the "twenty items or less" aisle out of fear of reprisals from her fellow shoppers, and moved down to aisle four. The woman and the young boy from earlier were checking out, and one elderly woman with a modestly filled basket was in line in front of them.

Madison assessed their haul and was pleased with herself. Behind her, the sounds of chaos ensued. At the entryway to the left of the checkout aisles, people tried to force their way through the sliding doors, causing a jam. A store employee attempted to assist the new shoppers and received a shove to the floor for her efforts.

Shouts and arguments filled the air from the aisles. The crash of broken glass caused a momentary silence before the mayhem continued. Madison was astonished at how quickly the situation devolved into pandemonium. As Alex slid the blue divider stick behind the elderly woman's stack of Ensure, Madison thought about how the behavior of human beings was so unpredictable. They were not wired to accept change very well. Their psyche was too sensitive. She wondered if it had always been that way, or was it because society was too coddled now and therefore unable to adapt.

Alex began to unload Madison's cart as a heavyset man rammed his shopping cart into her backside. Madison lurched forward and looked back at the man, who was obviously impatient. The line behind him had developed, and there were angry shouts demanding more open checkout lanes.

Ordinarily, Madison would try to monitor the prices as they were rung up on the electronic register system. Today, it was impossible to keep up. Although they had been in the store for nearly an hour at this point, it had been anything but a leisurely shopping day for mother and daughter. This trip reminded Madison of an episode of *Supermarket Sweep*, which had aired on Lifetime years ago.

Alex worked with the lone bagger to relocate the day's haul from the conveyer belt to the empty carts. The groceries, which filled two carts while in the store, now required three carts to depart the premises.

The bored and oblivious checkout clerk looked at Madison and asked, "Do you have your Kroger card with you today?"

"What?" asked Madison, clearly distracted from the normal shopping experience.

"Would you like your discount? Do you have your Kroger rewards card? If not, I can sign you—"

Madison interrupted the clerk as the man behind her slammed a case of Schlitz beer on the conveyor belt, causing her to jump. "Sorry, here."

"Your total is one thousand one hundred twenty-one dollars, thirty-four cents," announced the clerk.

Madison reached for her phone out of her bag and immediately noticed there were no missed calls or text messages from Colton. *I hope he's okay.* She navigated to the Chase Bank Mobile App, which was accepted by Kroger as payment. She scanned the phone to pay.

No response. She tried it again. Nothing.

"Is this machine working?" she asked, referring to the Canadian-based Moneris VX520 iTerminal mounted next to the register.

"It was," replied the clerk. "Try a credit card."

Madison, feeling the pressure from the probing eyes of the shoppers behind her, fumbled through her purse and found her wallet. The man behind her let out an audible sigh, followed by an obnoxious belch.

Madison found her Chase debit card and swiped it again.

Nothing. This time a message on the terminal read *Card Fail*.

Madison stared at the machine, dumbfounded. They had plenty of money in their bank account to pay for the groceries. Embarrassment was beginning to overwhelm her.

"It reads card fail," she whispered to the clerk, or so she thought. The man behind her lifted his now empty cart and dropped it to the floor with a loud clank.

"C'mon, let's go!" he huffed.

Madison ignored him and tried another card. Same result. *Card Fail*.

"There must be something wrong with your machine," said Madison. The clerk stared back at her with no expression or suggestion. A store manager interrupted the transaction with an announcement over the store's PA system.

"May I have your attention, please? Please, Kroger shoppers. May I have your attention? We are experiencing difficulty with our credit card processing company. At this time, we are only able to accept cash or check for payment."

Madison frantically waved Alex over. "Give me your checkbook."

"It's in my book bag. In the truck."

"Run out there and get it, sweetie," said Madison.

Alex leaned in to whisper to her mother, "Mom, I don't have that much money in my account. You do remember how much my allowance is, right?"

"Get it anyway. They'll never know. Now, hurry. Run!"

As Alex scampered off, Madison turned to the clerk. "My daughter is going to get the checkbook."

This brought roars of disapproval from the man behind her and several others, including a baby who was wailing uncontrollably.

"Get out of line!"

"Start over!"

"This is ridiculous!"

Madison tried to plead her case and buy time. "It's not my fault that the credit card machine doesn't work. My daughter will be right back. Just a moment more!"

The man behind her shoved his cart into Madison again. She was angry now.

Madison turned on the man and grabbed the front of his cart with both hands. "Stop hitting me with that cart!"

"Or what, lady?" he shouted back. "You're a hundred and forty pounds soakin' wet. What exactly are you gonna do, huh?"

Nothing, of course, but Madison was tired of being bullied by this crude guy. She was about to respond when one of the store managers appeared on the scene.

"What seems to be the problem here?" he asked.

"She ain't got no money!" shouted one of the people in line.

"Yes, I do have money," started Madison. "Your machine doesn't work and my daughter just ran to the car to get the checkbook. She'll be back any moment."

"Hey, me beer's gettin' hot!" shouted bully boy behind her.

The store manager glanced at the man and his beer before addressing Madison. "Ma'am, perhaps we should have you step aside so that we can keep the line moving."

Alex came running through the front entrance, holding the checkbook over her head.

"Here she comes. If you'll excuse me, I'd like to check out and leave now."

# CHAPTER 26

**9 Hours**
**2:02 p.m., September 8**
**Bank ATM**
**West End**
**Nashville, Tennessee**

They had to force their way past the throng of new shoppers who were shoving their way into the store. Madison glanced down the aisles as they pushed their three heavy carts toward the exit. Large sections of the shelves were empty. The floors were littered with broken or damaged groceries. Many customers carried what they could, as available shopping carts were at a premium. She immediately conjured up images of countries that had recently experienced economic collapse like Venezuela.

"Hey, I need one of your carts," said a man who followed them out of the store.

"Just a moment while we unload," replied Madison, who immediately felt apprehensive about the man following them to their truck. Despite being in broad daylight, she imagined the man carjacking their truck and kidnapping them or worse.

As their Suburban came into view, she was actually relieved to see the small red Kia that blocked them in. At least the man following them couldn't steal their truck. She'd figure out what to do with the offending KIA later.

The man, as it turned out, was a decent guy who wanted to secure a cart before going into the store. He needed diapers and formula for their newborn and knew he couldn't carry much. He helped the women lay down the backseat and moved Alex's golf clubs toward the front to make room for their groceries. He chatted briefly with her about golf and then was on his way. Madison closed the rear trunk lid and joined Alex inside. She immediately locked the doors, turned on the air conditioner, and caught her breath.

From their vantage point, they could see the melee, which best described the last senior shopping day to be held at Kroger for a long time. One woman, in a panic to pack her groceries into her small car, allowed her shopping cart to roll away, which included her kicking and screaming two-year-old. The cart almost crashed into a car that was waiting on her parking space. A Good Samaritan made the rescue, but unceremoniously lifted the two-year-old out, pointed her in the direction of the distraught mother, and ran into the store, pushing the cart to its limits.

Horns were blaring. A fistfight erupted over a stolen parking spot. Some cars were simply abandoned for lack of a better parking option, which brought Madison's attention back to the red KIA Soul.

The words of the rude man in the store came into her mind. *You're a hundred and forty pounds soakin' wet.* No, I weigh one twenty-eight, thank you. She looked at the KIA again.

"Alex, how much do you think that little car weighs?"

"I don't know, Mom," she replied as she scrolled through her Twitter feed.

Madison answered her own question. "I think about a ton. My guess is we're closer to three tons, maybe more."

"What's the point, Mom?"

"Well, I believe we've waited long enough for whoever this rude person is that blocked us in. It's time to go."

Madison put the transmission into low gear and inched forward until the massive front end of the Suburban towered over its smaller counterpart.

"Mom!" Alex yelled. "What are you doing?"

"We don't have time for this, Alexis." Madison gave the Suburban gas and began to push the KIA sideways. The tires on the smaller vehicle began to screech as it slid along the hot asphalt pavement. Several would-be shoppers stopped to watch the commotion.

Madison was undeterred. She continued to push the KIA until it began to turn at an angle. She stopped, backed up, and pushed toward the rear of the red Soul to create a wider gap. After several back-and-forth maneuvers, the opening became wide enough for the Suburban to fit through and Madison pulled off.

She caught Alex staring at her.

"What?"

"Well, aren't you gonna leave a note?" asked Alex.

"Nope. Besides, they wouldn't like what I had to say anyway. We need to go find an ATM."

It took them ten minutes to get out of the parking lot and another ten to cross the White Bridge Road intersection, which yielded three bank options. The Bank of America on the corner had a line out its front doors and the ATM line was empty. While waiting for the light to change, she saw several people walk up to the machine, express some form of disgust, and then leave or join the line of people trying to enter the bank. A security guard was doing his best to keep order, but in the one-hundred-degree heat, tempers easily flared.

She drove past SunTrust on the left, hoping the smaller, more obscure US Bank location was a better option. She was wrong. The line extended around the building into the parking lot. Madison waited to turn around at Saint Thomas West Hospital where Alex was born.

"Mom, from what I can tell, there hasn't been any formal announcement or emergency alert about the solar flare. I got a text from my friend Janie, who said school let out early and the golf match was canceled this afternoon."

"Try the news networks," said Madison. She wheeled the big SUV in a U-turn and headed back towards the SunTrust ATM. Alex tuned the radio to CNN, where two people were yelling at each other about whether the White House was being irresponsible by not making a statement. One of the talking heads claimed the President was acting calm and prudent. The other complained the President was out of touch by playing with her grandchildren during a time of national crisis. This elicited an angry retort by the other argumentative combatant, who contended no such crisis existed. *"The sun is shining, big deal,"* he exclaimed.

This exchange was indicative of why Madison was disgusted with politics. Everything was politicized. A tragic school or restaurant shooting quickly became a raging debate about gun control. The poor grieving families didn't even have a chance to learn if their loved one was dead or alive before the two sides draped themselves in the flag. While one side decreed that allowing illegal aliens to enter the country uninhibited was compassionate and the right thing to do, the other side was deemed to be racist because they disagreed. It was a never-ending battle of left versus right. Common sense took a backseat to it all.

Madison found a parking space at the bank despite the long ATM line. She instructed Alex to keep monitoring the news, and Madison also asked her to try to reach her dad again. She didn't want to alarm Alex, but Madison was genuinely concerned about her inability to reach Colton by phone. She had no idea if he was still at the Cowboys' complex or whether he was on a flight home. She hoped he'd caught a plane, which would explain his lack of contact with her.

While in line, she engaged in idle chat with some of the other bank customers. Incredibly, several people in line were unaware of the impending solar storm. Madison casually asked if anyone had heard about it, which piqued the interest of those within earshot. They immediately took to their smartphones to look for information.

Within a minute, everyone in line, starved for information, attempted to call friends and family. Conversations turned into panicked discussions about what it meant. One man suspected the worst-case *doomsday scenario,* as he put it. He summed it up as no power, no utilities, and no government. *Think* Mad Max, he surmised.

Those in line began to focus their attention on the person using the ATM. Madison could feel them pressing from the rear as the line grew longer. The bank's parking lot was full, as were the drive-thru tellers. *The word was spreading,* and it had been less than an hour since the cell phone alert was issued.

Madison wished that she had more than one debit card. The most she could withdraw in a given day was six hundred dollars. After her experience at Kroger, she decided that having some cash on hand was a good idea. She had checked her balance this morning, which was part of her daily routine.

When it was her turn, Madison nervously entered her PIN number incorrectly twice. The pressure of the day and the people behind her caused her to lose focus. On the third try, she succeeded. As the transaction was being completed, she opted for a written receipt, hoping it might provide her a clue as to whether Colton had made a similar withdrawal.

She stepped to the side of the ATM and read the printed balance. She quickly did the math in her head. Only her earlier purchases and the cash withdrawal appeared to have been taken out of their account. Colton had not used the card today. As was her habit, she counted the money dispensed by the ATM machine. Madison normally would do that before leaving the ATM, but the long line forced her out of her routine.

It also caused her to lose awareness of her surroundings. Suddenly, a man rushed her and tackled her to the ground. He was grabbing for the money she held tightly in her fist.

"Give me the money," he growled in Madison's ear, while pinning her down with his knee. Madison could feel blood dripping down her neck where her chin had struck a rock. He was grabbing at her wrist. When he grabbed her hand and bent it backward, she lost her grip and let go of the money. The twenty-dollar bills blew into the grass, bouncing aimlessly until they wedged against a row of liriope plants.

She tried to yell for help, but couldn't vocalize the words. The man crawled over her, his knees driving the air out of her lungs. As he scrambled for the money, which was now blowing along the grass toward the hedges, he kicked her in the face. Madison was stunned. *Why isn't somebody helping me?*

That was when she saw the bright reflection of steel, followed by a primal, guttural scream. Alex came at the man with a vengeance— and a sand wedge. Madison could hear the cracking of ribs as Alex drove the shiny, polished steel blade into the man's side with all of her might.

The man roared in pain but continued to grab for the money. Alex didn't hesitate. She raised the club again and drove it down onto his left forearm, resulting in an audible *CRACK!* The mugger had rolled onto his back, abandoning the quest for Madison's money and choosing to beg for mercy. He held his left arm up with his right, gesturing for Alex to stop.

She didn't. Alex swung again, crushing the man's left hand and severing one of his fingers, which barely hung on by its skin. The man was kicking the ground, trying to push himself into the bushes for protection. Alex went after him again. This time, she drove the club into the ground, barely missing his feet. The golf club shaft snapped, leaving her to hold the grip while the sand wedge blade was embedded in the sod. The man used this as his opportunity to escape.

Alex turned to her mother. "Mom, are you okay?" Alex was frantically trying to dial 9-1-1, to no avail. She turned her attention back to her mom.

Madison wiped the blood off her neck and then discovered her nose was bleeding as well. She got onto her knees and nodded. As she came back to her senses, she realized two things. First, their money was blowing around on the grass, prompting her to overcome the pain and crawl on all fours to retrieve it.

The second thing she realized was nobody got out of the ATM line to help her.

# CHAPTER 27

**9 Hours**
**2:24 p.m., September 8**
**Harding Place**
**Belle Meade, Tennessee**

Alex did her best to concentrate on the road as she drove her mother home. Even though Saint Thomas Hospital was right around the corner, her mom insisted that she was all right. She just wanted to take a shower or, better yet, a nice bath.

The traffic was at a standstill until Alex veered off Highway 100 and down Belle Meade Boulevard. The stately mansions stood high on the hill overlooking one of the most famous streets in Nashville. Unlike the chaos surrounding the last hour, Belle Meade looked like any other day. Lawn crews cut grass. A jogger, despite the sweltering heat, made his way along the tree-lined divided street. The mailman was dutifully stuffing mailboxes.

Madison threw the bloodied golf towel on the floor at her feet. She spoke for the first time since the attack. "Alex, I am so proud of you. You may have saved my life."

"I'm glad you're okay, Mom. I wish we had gone to the hospital. He kicked you in the head. Do you remember that?"

"Trust me, I'm feeling it," replied Madison.

"What if you have a concussion?" asked Alex.

"I don't, or at least I'm pretty sure I don't have one. My nose isn't broken either."

"Well, that's good. I'm pretty sure Daddy would be upset if your nose was crooked." Alex attempted to lighten the mood. She glanced over at Belle Meade Country Club as she turned onto Harding Place. There were golfers coming and going like any other Thursday afternoon.

"No doubt," said Madison. "Honey, again, thank you."

"I didn't save your life, Mom. But as Granddaddy would say, I did save you from a good old-fashioned butt whoopin'." The women laughed as they passed Mrs. Abercrombie, who was retrieving her mail. Somehow the appearance of the longtime resident getting her mail struck the Ryman women as odd under the circumstances. They didn't say another word until Alex turned on her left turn signal and slowly guided the large SUV through the very narrow stone columns adorned with iron security gates.

"Home sweet home," muttered Madison.

"Yeah, no kidding," added Alex. "I've got this, Mom. Why don't you check yourself out and get changed. But what should I do with all of this stuff. We don't have room in our pantry for it."

Alex hopped out and opened the rear hatch. She handed her mom the keys to unlock the house. Alex studied Madison's face one last time to make sure she didn't appear confused or dizzy. Although the two didn't talk much on the way home, her mom appeared alert and coherent. She wasn't nauseous and didn't seem sensitive to the bright, midday sun.

Last summer, one of her guy friends got hit in the temple with a golf club while horsing around, resulting in a concussion. Alex remembered what the paramedics were asking him before they took him to the hospital. She planned on keeping a close eye on her mom for the next couple of hours.

"Honey, why don't you organize everything on the dining room table," replied Madison. "I'd kinda like to take inventory to see what we have. Okay?"

"Sure thing," replied Alex, and then she added, "Mom, I love you."

"I love you too, Alex. Listen, I'm fine. Don't worry about me. But I have to tell you something. I haven't heard from your father in hours. I want to assume he's on a plane and will be home soon. He may be driving. But, honestly, I can't say for sure. I just thought you should know."

"He'll be fine, Mom. We'll all be fine."

# CHAPTER 28

**9 Hours**
**2:24 p.m., September 8**
**Interstate 30**
**East of Dallas, Texas**

Amazingly, the traffic through downtown Dallas was relatively light. Based upon the frenzied state of affairs at DFW, Colton imagined bumper-to-bumper, rush-hour-level traffic. While he was thrilled to be on the road, a six-hundred-and-fifty-mile trek across the southeast was going to be a challenge.

Finding Divine Car Rental open with available vehicles was a welcome sight, at first. Then he discovered his car rental options were limited and pricey. He had to choose between a Chevrolet Corvette and a Mercedes-Benz R350 crossover-style SUV. He opted for speed because he didn't plan on any additional passengers and his luggage was back at the hotel. There simply wasn't time to stop by the hotel and gather his belongings.

The other factor that would normally affect his decision making was the price—seven hundred dollars per day. He assured the clerk that his use of the Vette was strictly local, and he only needed it for a day. In Colton's mind, either it wouldn't matter in a day, or he would be facing one heckuva AMEX bill next month. He did chuckle to himself when he declined the loss damage waiver. If Madison and Alex were right, the Vette would be worthless by morning, with or without insurance.

He worked his way into the HOV lane without fear or compunction. He would be breaking a lot of laws in the next eight hours as he sped home to his girls. He'd be safe, of course, but he would not be a model citizen. He was racing against time, and time had a head start.

Colton finally cleared the bulk of the city's traffic after he crossed the Interstate 635 loop. He was doing eighty miles an hour by the time he crossed Lake Ray Hubbard, and Colton barely noticed the town of Rockwall on his left as he sped toward the piney woods and the rolling hills of East Texas.

He had never driven a Corvette before and vowed to buy one if Madison would let him. It was simply the perfect driving machine. The interior resembled the cockpit of a flight simulator he once toured at the FAA when he was a child. Every square inch had a purpose and was sculpted in luxury. Today, however, the GPS was wholly inadequate thanks to the incoming solar particles disrupting satellite communications.

Without a map, Colton would have to rely on memory at first until he could stop somewhere and pick up a few things. The most important item on his list was a cell phone charger. His, unfortunately, was back in the hotel room, leaving his cell phone dead.

He fiddled with the Apple CarPlay onboard touchscreen. There was a phone function, but he wasn't able to connect to a cell tower. Colton imagined that wireless providers were overwhelmed under the circumstances. The onslaught of calls by millions of Americans as they reached out to loved ones or to gather information was probably crushing the system.

Colton managed to pull up a local news station, which was airing *The Sean Hannity Show*. Hannity was providing an update on the solar flare.

*"So far we have nothing from the White House on what might be a life-changing event for the American people. We have discussed the devastating impact of an EMP on our nation's critical infrastructure for years, and neither this administration nor the one before it took any action. While they waste money on their pet social programs, our nation has been put at risk of the very thing we are facing today."*

Colton pushed the car up to over ninety miles an hour as traffic thinned to the occasional eighteen-wheeler. The westbound lane towards Dallas was much busier. He turned his attention back to the radio.

*"I am fortunate to have with us today former Speaker of the House Newt Gingrich. Mr. Speaker, thank you very much for joining us today. First, let me say that I hope you are safe and ready for what might be a devastating event in the history of this nation."*

*"Well, thank you, Sean, and I can assure you that Callista and I have been prepared for something like this for some time. Sean, I have stated many times that the detonation of a high-altitude nuclear-delivered electromagnetic pulse could damage our power grid, rendering it inoperable for years. Make no mistake, this solar storm has the same potential."*

*"Mr. Speaker, I have been waiting all day for this administration to address the American people about this solar event, and instead we get a photo op of Madame President playing soccer with the grandkids. Is she ever going to take the national security of this great nation seriously?"*

Colton slowed momentarily as a sheriff's patrol car headed westbound. The deputy never gave Colton a look. He wondered if police radar was adversely affected by the solar radiation.

Gingrich continued. *"Sean, not only could this deal a deathblow to our society, it could be the kind of catastrophe that ends civilization as we know it, and that's not an exaggeration."*

*"I agree, Mr. Speaker, and I know that is why you have focused on these threats dating back to your time in office."*

*"Sean, the reason I began focusing on this is there are very few events you can't recover from. You can recover from 9/11 or Pearl Harbor. This is really different."* Gingrich paused and the radio became silent for a few seconds. *"This solar storm can create such a collapse of our fundamental productive capacity that you could literally see civilization crash and tear itself apart—from within."*

Colton looked into his rear and side view mirrors. He glanced at the clock. It was 3:00. He eased the Corvette Stingray to just over one hundred miles an hour.

# CHAPTER 29

**8 Hours**
**3:00 p.m., September 8**
**Ryman Residence**
**Belle Meade, Tennessee**

Madison studied her face in the mirror and began to cry. Her chin had a gash reminiscent of her childhood days when she would fall off her bike, skinning up knees and elbows, but never her face. Madison was photogenic as a child and was once featured on the cover of a teen romance novel back in the day before half-naked men book covers became the norm.

During Madison's pageant days, her beautiful face was her greatest attribute. She was always self-conscious of her body, as most young women are. Ultimately, it was the requirement to participate in the swimsuit portion of the pageants that ended her quest for the title of Miss Teen Tennessee. Despite her natural beauty, she wasn't comfortable parading on stage in a swimsuit.

She gathered herself and wiped away her tears. Then she started laughing. Between the bruise on her cheekbone and the gash in her chin, she bore a strong resemblance to Angelina Jolie in the *Lara Croft: Tomb Raider* movie. In a way, today had been one of the most exciting days in her life, and certainly a memorable one. She'd found a strength she never knew she had.

She glanced out the window and saw her neighbor Christie Wren riding bikes with her two young daughters on the sidewalk. Madison wondered about people like Christie. Did they simply float through life, completely unaware of events that threatened their existence?

Madison realized she had been like the Christie Wrens of the world just forty-eight hours ago. Like most Americans, she took her life for granted in many respects, especially the relative safety she enjoyed. In a culturally and socially advanced society, you could go through life assuming that your fellow man wasn't going to harm you just for the sake of causing harm.

When the threat of terrorism hit the country, Madison became more aware of people who seemed out of place. Admittedly, she was very nervous on an airplane if people of Middle Eastern descent were onboard. Despite the enhanced security measures put into place by the government, there was always that doubt.

If she had to go into downtown Nashville at night to meet Colton for a function, her eyes would dart about, seeking safe havens if a black person approached her on the sidewalk. Madison would never admit these things to her friends for fear of being labeled a racist. Of course, she felt guilty about having these thoughts. But the old axiom *better safe than sorry* justified her actions.

Madison perused her closet and picked out one of her jogging suits. Somehow, she felt the need to run, although she doubted she would go anywhere. The adrenaline was still pumping through her body.

Today, she was shocked by her fellow man. *Nothing has happened yet, people!* But she'd seen the dark side of mankind and it frightened her. Aggression, panic, and indifference were on full display. As she replayed the attack at the ATM over and over while she bathed, the aspect of the entire event that revolted her the most was the apathetic attitude of the onlookers. Had it not been for the quick thinking of her brave daughter, she could've been more severely injured.

She was also upset with herself for letting her guard down. On a normal day, it might be safe to count the money after it was dispensed from an ATM. *Although not really.* But after their experience at the grocery store, doing it in broad view of everybody was stupid. It was a lesson learned, and she vowed to be more aware of her surroundings.

Feeling better, Madison slowly made her way down the stairs, shrugging off her pounding cheek and the rest of the soreness from the attack. She found Alex stretched out on the sofa, nose buried in her MacBook.

Alex slammed shut her computer and tossed it on the ottoman.

"What's that all about?" asked Madison.

She sat up and voiced her frustrations. "Mom, they're so stupid. Get this. My friends wanna come over and go swimming. Right now. The sun is about to fry our planet and these twits wanna come over for a pool party!"

"Honey, maybe they don't know what's goin'—"

"Oh, they know, Mom. Plus, I told them the latest update. They don't care. They think it's nothing. They're looking at it as an excuse to lay out of school."

Alex flopped herself back into the comfort of the leather sofa and crossed her arms in disgust. *She is far too serious for a teenager.* Madison studied her daughter for a moment and decided to change the subject. Alex was committed to getting ready for this, whatever *this* was. Madison decided to channel Alex's energy toward that goal.

"Hey, you wanna help me take inventory of our food and supplies? Also, we need to find your grandfather's shotgun. Whadya say?"

"Yeah, sounds good, Mom."

Madison was pleased that Alex perked up. She was worried Alex might have difficulty dealing with the attack. It was bad enough that she'd seen her mother get mugged, but Alex had beaten that man viciously with her golf club. It showed a violent streak in Alex that Madison had never seen before. "The last time I saw the shotgun, it was in the garage. Let's start there."

"Sounds good," said Alex. The Ryman women were on the hunt for the elusive shotgun which, to Madison's knowledge, had never been fired since she and Colton met. She hoped it was still out there somewhere.

Their garage was fairly neat, but not because Colton was an impeccable organizer. It was because he was not *handy*. Colton did not have the Mr. Fix-It gene typical of most members of the male species. He didn't repair cars. If it wouldn't start, he'd call AAA. He didn't cut grass. He hired Julio's crew to do that for him. Before they purchased this home, it was inspected, twice. All repairs had to be performed before closing. Then Colton purchased one of those home warranties that weren't worth the paper they were written on. The warranty gave him the peace of mind that if something went wrong, he or Madison could pick up the phone and schedule a repair.

It wasn't that Colton was lazy. On the contrary, he worked long, hard hours climbing to the top echelon of talent agents in the country. When he was home, he wanted to spend time with Madison and Alex—not fixing toilets or cutting grass.

Over time, however, every household accumulated *stuff*. Everything from unwanted Christmas gifts that you couldn't possibly re-gift to the fabulous croquet set that everyone enjoyed playing—once. Bicycles hung above their heads next to the boxes of Christmas decorations. The garage became less of a place to park your car and more of a glorified mini-storage unit.

"Got it!" exclaimed Alex as she pulled a dusty, brown leather gun case out of the Rubbermaid storage closet. She set the case on the garage floor and pulled out another hidden gem—a fishing pole.

"Hey, I remember that," said Madison. "There should be two more in there and a tackle box."

Alex rummaged around and found all three rods and reels. The green tackle box was at the bottom of the closet, along with some pull-on, waterproof fishing boots.

"Wow, we used these four summers ago," said Alex.

"When we spent two weeks at the Allens' place in West Tennessee, if I remember correctly, you and Chase spent all day fishing or doing *something*." Madison started laughing as she teased her daughter about her first love. The two kids were inseparable, and although Alex tried to hide it, she cried on the way home from Shiloh.

"We didn't do *something*, I mean anything. Chase tried to show off and chew tobacco. He got sick and threw up in the lake. Then he tried to kiss me. Ugh!"

"That vacation was very relaxing and we all had fun. Do you

remember your dad and Jake singing by the campfire at night?"

"Yeah, that was pretty neat. Very *Kumbaya.*" Alex and Madison laughed. Jake Allen was Colton's first big client. Like many country careers, Jake's started at a honky-tonk on Printer's Alley in downtown Nashville.

*Back to business.* Madison examined the fishing gear and opened the tackle box. It was barely used. She wasn't sure where they would fish, unless they had to, but the gear could be useful nonetheless.

More importantly, the gun was there, and it would help them establish some form of security in their home. She unzipped the case and carefully removed the Remington 870 shotgun. The gun was twenty-five years old but didn't look like it had aged a day in its life, as they say.

Madison knew nothing about how to handle a shotgun. Common sense told her two things—don't touch the trigger and point it away from people. She knew to check the safety. She looked near the trigger and found the black button secured to the trigger guard. She clicked it back and forth, revealing black to red to black. *Red, danger?* She made sure it was on black.

She set the shotgun on a workbench and looked inside the case once again. She found the *Model 870 Owner's Manual,* a dozen birdshot shells, and a cleaning kit. There was also a pair of shooting glasses and some earmuffs.

"Alex, help me gather up the gun stuff and we'll take it inside. I think I'll let your dad handle this part of the operation. Do you agree?"

"Duh," replied the teenager.

# CHAPTER 30

**7 Hours**
**4:00 p.m., September 8**
**Interstate 30**
**Texarkana, Texas**

As Colton raced up Interstate 30 towards Little Rock, his mind drifted as he assessed his life in Texas prior to moving to Tennessee. His father worked himself into the grave. He was the ultimate family provider, except in one respect—spending time with his wife and son. The Ryman family started their lives in Texas as oil men and cattle ranchers until the Great Depression, when the oil industry took a nosedive and the cattle ranches were decimated by drought.

Unable to find a job, Colton's grandfather, Walter Ryman, went off to war and fought in Patton's Third Army as it raced across France in the summer of 1944. The fighting was vicious throughout the cold winter leading into 1945, and then it got downright ugly. Corporal Ryman's tank corps was assigned to the 89<sup>th</sup> Infantry Division to lend support during an offensive in April 1945.

As the 89<sup>th</sup> pushed into central Germany, the locals began to tell the U.S. soldiers of a prison camp nearby. Rumors were rampant as Corporal Ryman's unit pressed the attack and approached the small town of Buchenwald. The German concentration camp they found was horrific. The atrocities, abuses, and killings were more than most men could take mentally. But Corporal Ryman persevered as he assisted the survivors to safety.

One of the survivors was a Romanian-born Jew named Elie Wiesel. He and Corporal Ryman became friends and stayed in touch throughout Wiesel's years as a writer, professor, and ultimately, the winner of a Nobel Peace prize. As a holocaust survivor, Wiesel saw the horrors his fellow man was capable of inflicting. He relayed these sentiments to Corporal Ryman, who in turn warned his children and grandchildren to never underestimate the depravity of man.

As a result of the lessons learned from Wiesel, through his grandfather, Colton became charitable. His pledge to give back included more than the expected ten percent tithes and offerings taught in church. He was instrumental in establishing the CMA foundation. Inspired by his love for music and using his influence as one of the top country music agents in the country, Colton organized benefit concerts, social meet and greets, and established grants for music education.

He also vowed to spend more time with his family than his father spent with his. He had achieved the pinnacle of his career, with the next step being a high-powered New York or Los Angeles agency. Overtures had been made the last few years, but he quickly shut them down. He made enough money to provide for his family. They were comfortable, much more so than most. Now, his goal was to delegate more to subordinates, thus freeing up his family time.

Colton was cruising along at nearly one hundred miles an hour as the interstate traffic remained sparse. This part of southwest Arkansas was desolate as he approached the town of Hope, birthplace of former President Bill Clinton and a darn good man, Mike Huckabee. His mind wandered to politics until he was snapped back to reality.

Like so many drivers, at times you didn't realize it, but while your mind wandered, your foot got heavier on the gas as you considered all of the life's complexities. Then—every driver dreaded seeing them—the flashing red and blue lights in your rearview mirror.

Colton was being pulled over. His heart sank in his chest, his palms began to sweat, and a sense of dread overcame his body. He was doing a hundred miles an hour!

Being pulled over by the police was never a pleasant experience, but Colton, a skilled negotiator, immediately composed himself. While he knew there was no way to talk the trooper out of a ticket, he planned on doing his best to keep from going to jail. The last thing he needed was a delay or, worse, being locked up when the lights went out.

Colton immediately turned on his emergency flashers to let the officer know he'd seen his lights. He reached for his license, his GEICO insurance card, and the Destiny car rental contract. He was going to be a model of cooperation. Colton looked into his side view mirror and saw the Arkansas State Trooper approach his door cautiously, one hand on his service weapon.

Colton understood the officer's trepidation. In recent years, there had been a war on law enforcement officers. There were recent ambushes in Dallas, Baton Rouge, and Minneapolis, resulting in several murdered officers. Even during routine traffic stops, sudden and violent attacks were common. Dozens of highway patrol troopers were killed each year by gunfire, not to mention the fact they were hit by negligent drivers of passing vehicles.

After rolling down his window, Colton turned off the engine and placed both of his hands on the top of the steering wheel in plain view. His license and paperwork lay on the dash for the officer to see. Colton stayed calm and did everything he could to let the officer know he was not a threat. The lesson he learned from all the violence around the country involving law enforcement was this—comply with the officer's commands, and nobody gets hurt. It was that simple.

The trooper was a very large black man, who quickly filled up the side mirror's view. He positioned himself next to Colton's door and looked into the passenger seat. Then he spoke.

"You look like a pretty smart guy," he started. "Normally I'd ask *do you know why I pulled you over*. Somehow, I think you know the answer to that—one hundred miles an hour. Would you like to tell me what the hellfire emergency is?"

Colton glanced at the trooper's badge and saw his name—McKay. *Let's get personal.* "Trooper McKay, I know I was speeding and I'm sorry. Honestly, I'm trying to get home to my wife, Madison, and our daughter, Alexis, before this solar storm hits. The news has me worried about the power going down, and I'm concerned about them being home alone."

The trooper hesitated for a moment and glanced into the vehicle. "Do you have any weapons?"

"No, sir."

"Are you under the influence of alcohol or drugs, prescription or otherwise?"

"No, sir."

"Are those your credentials?"

"Yes. This is a rental car. I have my license and insurance card here as well."

Colton slowly reached for the paperwork on the dash and handed it out the window to the officer. The officer studied them for a moment and then handed back the insurance card.

"Mr. Ryman, I need you to exit the vehicle slowly and come with me."

*Darn it! He's gonna arrest me. Should I try to plead my case? Explain again how important it is to get home?* Colton's mind raced, and then he decided to follow the trooper's instructions.

"Sir, I need you to stand behind your vehicle, facing it. I'll be back with you in a moment."

Colton stood in the sweltering heat for a couple of minutes, unaware of the trooper's intentions. If he was arrested, at least he'd get a phone call to let Madison know he was okay. Cars were flying by, causing the Corvette to shake from the turbulence. Waiting on the trooper seemed like an eternity, but at least he wasn't handcuffed in the backseat of the Dodge on the way to the hoosegow.

*CRACK! CRACK! CRACK!*

The sound of gunfire caused Colton to instinctively duck and then lay flat on the hot asphalt pavement. He was momentarily disoriented as to the source of the noise. He looked under the Vette to see if he could hide there.

*CRACK! CRACK! CRACK!*

More gunshots. He caught a glimpse of two pickup trucks roaring down the westbound lane of the interstate. The passengers were hanging out of the windows, shooting at each other.

Colton scrambled to the far side of his car, digging his knees into the hot asphalt, which tore holes in his pants and bloodied his knees. The highway patrol car roared to life. Loose gravel spun from his tires and the smell of burning rubber filled Colton's nostrils as Trooper McKay chased bigger prey.

After a few seconds of profuse sweating on the pavement, Colton stood and looked around. *What the heck just happened?* He dusted himself off and looked at his bloody knees showing through his pants. For a moment, Colton debated whether to wait for the trooper to return with his driver's license or continue on his way.

Decision made. Colton was on the road again. He unbuttoned his shirt and turned all of the air vents in his direction so he could cool down. Turning off the adrenaline, however, was another matter. His heart was racing. People were shooting at each other on the highway, and he was doing a hundred miles an hour again after being stopped five minutes ago!

As he approached Hope, he decided to stop for gas, even though the tank had a hundred miles or more left in it. He could stop here, grab some water and munchies and maybe a change of clothes. The big blue Walmart sign at exit thirty provided him a pretty good option—until he reached the top of the exit ramp at Hervey Street.

Traffic was backed up in both directions. It would take forever to cross over the highway to get into Walmart. It appeared the entire town of Hope, Arkansas, was en route to their local Walmart. Colton looked to his right and saw an Exxon station. Cars were lined up onto Hervey, waiting their turn to pump gas. Some drivers stood outside their open car doors, with their hands on their hips. Several people waited in line, holding gas cans.

As Colton veered onto the shoulder of the exit ramp and began to back down the ramp to re-enter the interstate, he thought of a quote from church when he was a boy.

*When the world says give up, hope whispers—try it one more time.*

# CHAPTER 31

**7 Hours**
**4:00 p.m., September 8**
**Ryman Residence**
**Belle Meade, Tennessee**

For the better part of an hour, Madison and Alex watched news reports from around the country. The White House issued a brief statement stating they were monitoring the situation and first responders were prepared for every eventuality. The constant stream of images and news reports portrayed a different picture.

Society was collapsing. Long gas lines were shown, which included iPhone-filmed fistfights. Citizens' recordings and hidden cameras had changed the media landscape. Eyewitness videos were everywhere. These videos often created a narrative that could be manipulated by the media and politicians alike. In a way, these videos, without providing proper context, could cause a lot of harm.

But one thing was certain, in American society, everyone loved to watch a train wreck. America was at the beginning of an action-packed disaster film in the making. Sensationalist journalism was on full display. Both CNN and Times Square established a *Countdown to Impact Clock*. At midnight eastern time, 11:00 p.m. in Nashville, the clock would reach zero and impact would supposedly occur. Alex, a fifteen-year-old who had a way with words, decried the countdown clock as stupid. Nobody knew the precise moment a solar storm could hit Earth—*it was too big!*

Of course she was right, and the media knew this as well. But the clock created a sense of drama that kept viewers' eyes glued to CNN and its sponsors' messages.

Some of the news broadcasts were informative. Madison learned Earth barely missed being hit by a massive electromagnetic pulse burst from the sun in 2012. If that storm had hit the planet directly, the result would have been catastrophic. The scientists on the panel of guests hypothesized the current threat to be far greater than the 2012 event.

In addition to the most common predictions of radio blackouts and power outages, one economist talked extensively about the impact on the world's economy. A Lloyd's of London representative concluded the losses to be in the trillions of dollars. The rebuilding effort of the financial markets could take a decade.

Another guest was warning of a technological armageddon. Madison turned up the volume to hear his thoughts.

*"An electromagnetic pulse, whether man-made or caused by a solar flare, can range from a minor inconvenience to an extinction-level event. It just depends on how powerful it is."*

*"What can we expect?"* asked the host.

*"In the worst-case scenario, we could be facing a situation where our electrical grids have been fried, there is no heat for our homes, our computers don't work, most vehicles won't run, financial markets will close, hospitals are unable to function, nobody can pump gas, and supermarkets cannot operate because there is no power and refrigeration. Basically, we would witness the complete and total collapse of the economy and society,"* the guest responded.

*"How would the EMP affect humans?"*

*"The health impacts are negligible, by comparison, to the overall impact on human life. According to the government-created EMP commission, ninety percent of the U.S. population would die from starvation, disease and societal chaos within one year of a massive EMP attack. It would be a disaster unlike anything mankind has experienced in history."*

Madison hit the mute button and looked at Alex to see if this revelation induced a reaction in her. Apparently, it did not. This was a lot to heap on the shoulders of any teenager, whose lives were typically all about perceived drama. Alex, mature for her age, was unfazed.

"Mom, we should fill up the bathtubs, sinks, and every available container with water." She jumped off the couch and headed upstairs. "You start in the kitchen, okay?"

"Uh, sure," replied Madison. This certainly made sense and Madison was antsy. They should be doing something, not sitting around watching the same news reports repeatedly—*or anxiously waiting for Colton to come home or at least call.*

As she filled water containers throughout the house, she made one last phone call to her mother. It was too late for her to catch a flight to Nashville, and she assured Madison that she had an excellent support group. Her circle of friends in Siesta Key, both male and female, were elderly but feisty. They would take care of each other like family.

Empty glasses now stood full of water. Likewise, Tupperware, flower vases, mixing bowls, and even the mop buckets became storage containers for the most important ingredient of life—water.

Madison turned her attention to their food supply. Alex had organized their grocery purchases on their eight-foot-long, carved oak dining table. Food from the pantry was on display as well. She placed cleaning supplies on the floor next to the outside wall, and personal hygiene supplies were clustered together in one corner.

"Wow," Madison muttered aloud. "Where do I start?" She thought back to a passage she'd read on that author's website. For the beginning prepper, he suggested you think about your everyday life—from the time you wake up in the morning until you sleep at night. *Consider the things you do as part of your everyday routine.*

*Remember the Prepper Rule of Threes,* he admonished. *Three is two, two is one, and one is none. After the end of the world as we know it, or TEOTWAWKI, Walmart and Target will be closed. You either have what you need, or you will have to forage and barter for those items. Both of those activities are fraught with risk.*

*For example, many people brush their teeth first thing in the morning. Make sure you have a toothbrush, toothpaste, and a backup for each.* Madison thought about her routine. Well, the first thing she did was use the bathroom. That required toilet paper. Ugh! What if they didn't have any more toilet paper.

Madison ran into the kitchen and grabbed a notepad and pen. She began making a list.

*Toothpaste. Toothbrushes. Toilet paper!*

The next thing she would do was have breakfast. She looked at the dining table covered with food and considered the most nutritious, easy-to-fix meals for breakfast.

*Cereal. Oatmeal. Sugar. Honey. Powdered milk.*

As part of her morning routine, after she ate, she would take her vitamins, peruse the news headlines online, and enjoy a cup of coffee.

*More vitamins. Coffee. Powdered creamer. Herbal tea bags.*

Madison thought about her laptop sitting on the kitchen table in the mornings, unplugged. She immediately ran around the house, plugging in all of the electronic devices so they would be fully charged. What else?

The compressor of the freezer in the kitchen kicked on. Yes! She opened both refrigeration units and turned their levels to maximum. This might add an extra few hours of chill to the food inside. *We'll not worry about energy savings today.*

"Mom," Alex asked as she came down the stairs, "do we have a portable radio? You know, like the old days?"

Crap! They needed some kind of weather radio or at least a small handheld AM radio like people used at sporting events.

*Portable radio. Batteries.*

"I'm making a list, honey," replied Madison. "We don't have one that I know of."

"Whadya want to eat for dinner?" asked Alex, staring into the pantry. "Should we cook something or just munch on something in the fridge."

*Cooking! I forgot. How are we going to cook this stuff?* They had a propane grill, but they could use something more portable—like campers used. What about cast iron?

*Portable camp grill. Cast iron. Aluminum foil. Heavy-duty oven mitts.*

Alex entered the dining room as Madison continued to scribble notes on the list.

*Basic tool kit. Tea kettle or campfire coffee pot. Gas can, with gas.*

"Mom, why are you making a list? Amazon probably won't be delivering tomorrow."

Madison caught her breath and brushed the hair out of her face. She was sweating. She looked at Alex and contemplated the risks and dangers of going back out.

The store shelves might be empty. Places like Kroger, Publix and Walmart would be so full of shoppers that they could get trampled to death. Madison thought of alternatives that might not be on other people's radar.

But even then, she replayed the events at the store and ATM from just two hours ago. She glanced at the images filling the screen on CNN. People were going crazy! Other drivers would be dangerous. Looters might be out already. They could get robbed, at gunpoint this time.

Madison studied the list. Were the items written down worth risking her life and her daughter's? She looked into the mirror hanging on the dining room wall and lifted her chin to show the scabbed wound. Madison winced slightly as she pushed against her bruised cheek, causing the skin to turn momentarily white before returning to its new shade of purplish red. She made a decision.

*Life isn't about steering clear of peril. It's about making calculated risks and then going all in.*

She had to do something. She needed to do all she could to get ready.

"We're goin' on a run," announced Madison.

Alex shrugged nonchalantly and said, "Okay. Can we get pizza?"

# CHAPTER 32

**7 Hours**
**4:40 p.m., September 8**
**ALMA**
**Atacama, Chile**

Dr. Stanford sat back in a chair, twirling the end of a pen in her mouth. Only a few members of the JAO Team remained at their stations. Some of the scientists were trying to catch a plane out of the coastal city of Antofagasta on the Pacific Ocean to their native countries. The team's projections spared ALMA and countries closer to the equator from the grid-destroying effects of the G5 geomagnetic storm. Dr. Stanford agreed that if the storm took out the electric grid this close to the center of the planet geographically, the world would be facing an extinction-level event.

Her dutiful assistant, Jose, remained by her side throughout the day. He was a workhorse, especially when it came to dealing with the various world governments that relied upon her forecasts. Dr. Stanford knew he was exhausted and urged him to take a nap on the sofa in her office. He declined, as she knew he would.

Like Dr. Stanford, Jose had been fascinated by the sun as the giver of life. A devout Catholic, Jose was in awe at the position of the earth and the perfect orbital distance from the sun to sustain life. In his mind, only God could have created this wondrous planet and all forms of life that inhabited it.

Jose was careful to avoid debates about religion and science with his colleagues. He learned early on that the majority of his peers were nonbelievers, and there was nothing he could say to convince them otherwise. To him, the miracles provided by God were amazing, and he didn't want to complicate his faith by someone else's scientific view.

Dr. Stanford had conversations with Jose when he was first elevated to his position. She respected his point of view and promised not to impose her scientific way of thinking upon him. She grew up fascinated by the magnificence of the sun like he did. Their childhood shaped their lives, and now they were able to work side by side without the complications of religious beliefs affecting their working relationship.

"Jose, we've got the best seat in the house," said Dr. Stanford. "As long as the satellites don't get blasted out of orbit, we'll be able to see the impact of this G5 in all its glory."

"It will be historic, Dr. Stanford," he added.

"Look at this," said one of the JAO Team. Dr. Stanford and Jose turned their attention to his array of monitors, which produced satellite imagery of X-rays, magnetic energy, and temperature tables. He pointed to one of the monitors. "Check out the magnetogram. Look at these readings along the sun's surface."

Dr. Stanford studied the monitor. An area on the west limb of AR3222 showed a brilliant plume of plasma erupting from the surface.

"Another one," she muttered.

"It might loop," said Jose, referring to the sun's habit of bending much of its escaped magnetic energy back into its coronal opening. "That said, even with a loop, it will likely shoot an electromagnetic pulse our way."

"The earth's magnetosphere will be weakened by this first blast," said Dr. Stanford. "A second CME of the same magnitude may have a damaging radiation effect on the latitudes nearest the poles."

The group continued to study the magnetogram. The bulging loop of the solar flare held onto the solar disk like a drop of water from a leaky kitchen faucet. The loop, filled with helium and hydrogen particles, did not close and return to the sun under its intense gravitational pull as Jose predicted. It kept rising from the surface, swelling like a balloon about to pop. As the solar flare's footprint grew, both across the solar disk and into space, it became apparent it would not be contained.

The solar plume grew, and then it released toward the earth at three million miles an hour. Like the massive flare that was headed their way, this X-flare would gain steam with the solar wind, and its charged particles would follow in the wake of the X58 scheduled for full impact on the earth's atmosphere in just over six hours.

"*Dios mío, con espalda con espalda,*" said Jose.

"That's right, Jose," translated Dr. Stanford. "Back-to-back."

"Should I call it in?" asked Jose.

"Let's finalize our predictive model," Dr. Stanford replied. "Realistically, this geomagnetic storm will be secondary to the damage caused to the power grids of those nations affected by the X58. My concern relates to the potential collapse of Earth's magnetosphere, even if for a short time. If this new CME chases the X58, this is not a minor situation. The blast of heat energy can trigger earthquakes, volcanic eruptions, and unpredictable ocean currents. We're talking real climate change here."

Dr. Stanford tapped her associate Deb Daniels on the shoulder and instructed her to pull up the BATS-R-US model. The computer model used an adaptive grid program that allowed it to create an infinite number of calculations upon the elements of solar wind plasma—density, velocity, and temperature.

She began to bring up numbers and showed Dr. Stanford the results. She gave Daniels further instructions. "Now, plug the models into the SWMF—the Space Weather Modeling Framework."

Everyone in the room had joined the trio as they watched the results come on screen. The room was deathly silent.

"That's what I was afraid of," started Dr. Stanford. "We might experience a geomagnetic excursion."

"Excursion?" questioned Jose.

"Yes," started Dr. Stanford. "A geomagnetic excursion is a significant shift in Earth's magnetic shield, just like a geomagnetic reversal. Unlike reversals, an excursion does not permanently change the large-scale orientation of the field."

"Does it flip the poles?" asked a member of the JAO Team.

The pole-shift hypothesis suggested that in the past, there had been geologically rapid shifts in the relative positions of the north and south poles as they related to the axis of the Earth's rotation. These pole shifts were deemed responsible for triggering tsunamis, earthquakes, and volcanic activity near the tectonic plates.

While there were scientific studies indicating that the poles did wander, the studies did not lend credence to the theory that a rapid shift was possible. These shifts took many years. However, the studies were all based upon speculation due to lack of hard scientific data. The potential was real, it just hadn't occurred in modern times.

"In the case of a geomagnetic excursion," started Dr. Stanford, "there is a dramatic, typically short-lived decrease in field intensity, with a variation in pole orientation as much as forty-five degrees."

"What's the impact on Earth's geomagnetic field?" asked Jose.

"The last geomagnetic excursion occurred forty thousand years ago, during the last Ice Age. It was called the Laschamp Event. Based upon radiocarbon dating analysis, the reversed field was seventy-five percent weaker."

"So these things happen," interrupted Jose. "But does it necessarily result in a mass extinction?"

"The danger is the substantially elevated levels of radiation for years to come," continued Dr. Stanford. "An analysis of the Laschamp Event revealed substantially greater production of beryllium-10 and carbon-14. Carbon-14 is the radioactive isotope that is emitted from nuclear power plants."

"How does this relate to the weakening of Earth's magnetic field as the X58 hits the planet tonight?" asked one of the scientists.

"Due to the weakening of the magnetic field, particularly during the impact period, another major geomagnetic storm would allow greater amounts of radiation to reach Earth, increasing production of the radioactive isotopes beryllium-10 and carbon-14," replied Dr. Stanford.

She wandered to the entry and stared at a wall of enlarged

photographs featuring images of wildlife along the Chilean coastal regions.

"Some forms of migratory life that are thought to navigate based on magnetic fields may be disrupted. These species may or may not be able to adjust, although some of these species have survived excursions in the past."

"Will the biggest impact be seen at the poles?" asked Jose.

"Since geomagnetic excursion periods are not always global, any effect might only be experienced in certain places, with others relatively unaffected," replied Dr. Stanford. She thought about the potential duration of such an event, and then added, "The time period involved could be as little as a human lifetime or as much as ten thousand years."

"What would the effect be on people?" asked another scientist.

"Increased ultraviolet radiation will result in a variety of skin cancers, including the life-threatening melanoma," replied Dr. Stanford as she continued to stare at the photographs. "For the eyes, cataracts are likely to develop, as well as conjunctiva, a malignant cell cancer. Then there is a suppression of our immune system. UV exposure will enhance the risk of infection and decrease the effectiveness of vaccines."

"None of this is good," interjected Jose.

As Dr. Stanford returned to the group, she walked up to the monitors and leaned over them. She studied the ever-changing numbers and the pulsating images of the sun.

She summed it up, taking a deep breath before speaking. "It will all depend on the speed of the second CME. Guys, now we have something else to watch. The first wave may knock us against the ropes—robbing us of our power, but the second wave may knock us out."

# CHAPTER 33

**7 Hours**
**4:40 p.m., September 8**
**West End**
**Nashville, Tennessee**

"I still think we should take the gun," said Alex as Madison approached the intersection of Harding Pike. This portion of US 70 South stretching toward Bellevue was far less crowded than the White Bridge Road intersection a few miles closer to town.

"We don't know how to use it, for one thing, and we won't be long." Madison inched forward as the traffic ahead of them moved through the green light. As Walgreen's parking lot came into view on her left, she saw a line of cars stretching around the building. The drive-thru pharmacy window was overwhelmed.

But this turned out to be a blessing because other potential shoppers avoided the store on the premise that it was too busy. Unlike pharmacies of years past, Walgreen's and their counterpart CVS had become more about selling sundries and household items and less about dispensing prescription medications.

They parked the Suburban and walked briskly across the parking lot. By 4:30, the sun had heated up Nashville to one hundred one degrees, which was another record if such things were worthy of discussion on a day when the Sun planned on dealing a death blow to the planet. They dashed between two of the cars standing in line and entered the store, finding it surprisingly empty.

Alex immediately noticed the *cash only, no checks* sign and brought Madison's attention to it. *Figures.* They'd scraped together every piece of loose change in the house. Alex had even retrieved a twenty-dollar bill out of her golf bag, which was there for emergency money. With their seven-hundred-and-eighty dollars, the two shoppers would have to be frugal. The big-ticket items, if they were available, would be found at their next two stops.

Madison produced the list and the two got to steppin'. Personal hygiene and additional overlooked grocery items were the top priority. Madison grabbed more vitamin and nutritional supplements. Finally, she grabbed a couple of boxes of Walgreen's Stay Awake Caffeine tablets. The three of them would have to establish a round-the-clock security rotation. Caffeine could help them stay awake until their bodies adjusted to the midnight shift.

While Alex was checking out, Madison ran back to the pharmacy counter and found three last minute items—a digital thermometer, an inexpensive blood pressure unit, and a glucose monitor. The last item, oddly enough, came to mind when she saw the pool water-testing equipment. Their eating and sleeping habits would change dramatically. She thought it might be a good idea to monitor their blood sugar.

She added the items to the pile and Alex held up several packages and asked, "What are these?"

"Mylar blankets," replied Madison.

"They look like aluminum foil. Are they like the balloons?"

"Same material, but they'll keep us warm if we get stuck out somewhere. People put them in their medical kits."

Some of the other items Madison picked up were hand warmers, lighters, matches, two manual can openers, and some baby wipes.

"Your total is two hundred and seventeen dollars, fifty cents."

Madison counted out eleven twenties and handed the money to the clerk. She noticed the store had filled up while they were shopping. Taking her change, she thanked the clerk and headed for the exits. Walgreen's knocked out a big part of their list.

After they had loaded the SUV, Madison shot across the street to Hart's Ace Hardware. The family-owned store had been a fixture in Nashville for nearly seventy years. Alex was a classmate with one of the Hart boys in grade school.

As she pulled into the parking lot, she glanced to the front of the building to confirm that they still had some standard, twenty-pound propane tanks used for most barbecue grills. She also hoped to find a more portable propane grill just in case mobility became necessary.

The store only had a handful of customers. A small retail hardware store was looked over by most of today's frenzied shoppers. As she entered the store, she noticed the handwritten *BROKEN* sign taped to the credit card machine. She casually asked the clerk if she would accept a check since the machine was out of service. The answer was yes, and the items on Madison's list just grew significantly.

"Outstanding, Alex. Let's get started."

Madison began to walk towards the outdoor living area in search of a camping grill when she suddenly stopped to ask the clerk a question. "Do you have any generators?"

"We only have one left. It's a Generac Tri-Fuel for six hundred eighty-nine dollars."

"Tri-fuel?" asked Alex.

"Triple fuel," replied the clerk, adding, "they operate on gasoline, natural gas, and propane."

Madison didn't hesitate. "We'll take it. Set it aside for us, and add two tanks of propane too. Okay?"

"You got it," replied the young woman.

Madison and Alex both grabbed a cart and hustled toward their lawn and garden department.

"Good job, Mom."

"Why, thank you! Now, let's find something more portable to cook on." They found a Camp Chef modular cooking system that provided two burners. Madison added a Wenzel three-person tent to the cart, and then sent Alex back up front for another cart.

They moved through the store and quickly added items on the list, and a few that were not, including a variety of knives. She found an Eton Solar Crank emergency radio, several styles of flashlights, and batteries to power them all. She also grabbed a solar charger that could handle smartphones, iPads, flashlights and other electronic devices.

The last two items, which the girls had to carry, were ten-gallon galvanized trash cans with lids. A roll of 3M aluminum tape finished off her list.

"Mom, really?" asked Alex, holding them up in each hand. "Are we going *industrial* with our home décor?"

"Ha-ha, very funny." Madison laughed. "When we get home, I'll show you. Your beloved iPod will thank me as well."

A helpful ACE hardware man, unlike the more modern, politically correct ACE hardware person, arrived on the scene to help them check out. He escorted them to the parking lot to assist with the loading of the generator and other items into their truck.

After he closed the deck lid, Madison thanked him and then asked, "Do you know where Nashville Gun and Knife is located? It's supposed to be close by."

"It is," he answered, "but it's closed. They stopped by here as they were going out of town."

"Out of town?" asked Madison.

"Yeah, they have a place on the Cumberland Plateau. They're gonna ride out this solar storm over there."

"Aren't you worried about it?" asked Alex.

"Young lady, the Hart family has lived here for nearly a century. I'm seventy-eight years old. I'm not goin' anywhere, and neither is this hardware store. If somethin' happens, then we'll just set us up the Hart Family Trading Post."

The three of them laughed and Alex spontaneously hugged the man. They smiled at each other and he slowly walked back inside with his hands in his pockets, looking around the exterior of the store with pride.

"Mom, what did you plan on buying at the gun store?" asked Alex as the two entered the truck.

"I was gonna give it a try. You know, buy a used gun under the table, sort of."

"It would've been worth a try." Alex shrugged.

Madison was about to turn onto Harding Place, pleased with their haul, when she accelerated through the light instead.

"Hang on," said Madison.

"Where are we going?"

"I've got an idea," replied Madison, and she pulled into Phillips Toy Mart.

"Toys, really, Mom?" Alex started to thumb through her Facebook news feed.

"Just a hunch, wait here and lock the door. Also, pay attention."

Madison jumped out of the truck and went inside. She approached a bored clerk, who was also scrolling through one of her social media accounts. To save time, Madison asked her if she had any toy guns or BB pistols.

Without looking up, the indifferent clerk pointed toward the rear of the store and said back wall. Madison found a wall section of Daisy and Crosman products. She bought a Crosman Airsoft rifle, which resembled an AR-15, and two Taurus PT-111 look-alike BB pistols. She didn't bother with the BBs, as that was not the purpose of these *tools*.

On the way to the checkout, she grabbed some black model spray paint. Madison, frustrated at her inability to acquire real weapons, did the next best thing—she improvised. The BB guns she purchased were realistic replicas. With the spray paint, she could cover the distinctive bright orange muzzle tips if they couldn't be removed altogether. If the situation arose, the Rymans could bluff their way out of a potentially deadly standoff.

# CHAPTER 34

**6 Hours**
**5:22 p.m., September 8**
**West End**
**Nashville, Tennessee**

Things had gone too smoothly. Madison and Alex were very pleased with the items they picked up in the three stores. A little over an hour ago, they'd traveled this route from their house, past Belle Meade Country Club, and encountered very little traffic.

When she reached a Metro Nashville police officer, he refused to provide them an explanation and told her she'd have to turn around and find another way to her destination. Belle Meade Boulevard was closed. When Madison pressed him for more answers, he became angry and actually placed his hands on his service weapon. This frightened Madison, and she immediately maneuvered the Suburban into a three-point turn and headed back to US 70 South.

"This is stupid," said Alex. "Our house is less than two miles from here. We have to go all the way around Belle Meade."

"It is stupid, but I don't know that we have a choice. It's getting late, and I really wanted to get home and settled before dark. I'm sure your dad will be home soon too." Madison pulled into the parking lot at Harding Academy and thought for a moment. She could go left a few miles and work her way around Percy Warner Park, then back up north on Hillsboro Pike. Or about a mile up, she could catch Woodmont Boulevard over to Green Hills and come down that way. They still had several hundred dollars available. There might be a store open that could add to their supplies.

"What's the plan, Mom?"

"It'll be shorter to go up and over," she replied. "We'll head back up to the scene of the crime and then take Woodmont over to Green Hills. Madison pulled out onto US 70 and navigated north toward the Kroger store where they had shopped earlier in the day. At the Belle Meade Boulevard entrance, several police cars blocked the road, and traffic came to a standstill as people rubbernecked the scene. Alex stretched her neck to look down the street.

"I see that yellow crime scene tape. It's stretched across the road about one hundred and eighty yards down."

As a talented golfer, Alex was very accurate on distances within three hundred yards. Madison followed the traffic and inched toward the Woodmont interchange. After twenty minutes, she realized she'd made a mistake and wanted to do a U-turn towards Percy Warner Park. But now the traffic on the southbound side was bumper-to-bumper. *What a mess!*

Madison was blocked in and couldn't move. She decided a last stop in the Green Hills area was out of the question. She should've known—*pigs get fat, hogs get slaughtered.* At this point, she focused on getting them home safely. Lynnwood was just ahead. She'd turn right there and work her way through the neighborhoods to their house. Suddenly, her adventure was becoming a chore.

A young man startled Alex by beating on her window, causing her to shriek.

"Hey, ladies! How are you this fine day?" said another man, who was grabbing the roof rack of their truck and shaking it. Madison looked around and immediately wondered where they came from.

Her first reaction was to honk the horn. She wanted the cars in front of her to move so she could get away from the thugs. The loud blast had no effect on the surrounding vehicles, but it did seem to anger a third man who joined his friends. He was wearing a bandana as a mask around his mouth. The image on the bandana resembled a skull.

One of the men stood on the side rail and attempted to open the rear passenger door, causing Madison to panic. She lurched the

Suburban forward, almost hitting the bumper of the Toyota in front of her. As she did so, the man on Alex's side of the truck flew off onto the pavement and rolled into the curb.

Madison quickly weighed her options. She was blocked in on the left side, front and rear by cars—many of whom joined in the frustration by slamming on their horns. There was a three-foot-tall slave fence erected along the open field to their right, but it had withstood one hundred fifty years of traffic, from horses to vehicles.

First used by Scottish immigrants in the eighteenth century, slave fences sprouted up all over the country as a way of creating a barrier to hold livestock. If a farmer's cattle got out and caused damages, they would be held liable. On a second offense, the farmer would have to pay double damages. They were built to last.

Madison was afraid to tear up the drivetrain or flatten a tire by ramming through it. Her only option was to bull her way down the shoulder, except for the fact that a lamppost stood in the way.

"Mom, what are we gonna do? They're not leaving."

"I don't know, can you—"

But Madison was startled by one of the men, who used the tire to catapult himself onto the hood of their car. He began jumping up and down, waving his arms and hollering, "It's the end of the world! The end is near! Woo-hoo!"

Now Madison was pissed. She threw the truck into reverse, and the man lost his balance, bounced on his back, and rolled off the hood of the Suburban to the ground. He tried to regain his balance and stand up, but fell against the trunk lid of the Toyota in front of them.

For the second time that day, Madison used her bumper. She slowly inched forward and pinned the man to the back of the Toyota. The Toyota driver rolled down his window and started waving his arms.

Now the hoodlums were frightened. They were running around the front fenders of the Suburban, banging on the hood of the SUV, shouting for Madison to back up.

"Mom! You'll kill him!" Alex was frantic. She leaned up in her seat and looked over the hood at the man, who appeared to be losing consciousness.

"Why shouldn't I?" asked Madison. Just as she was about to put the Suburban in reverse, the Toyota driver spun the tires and lurched forward, which unpinned the thug. He fell onto the pavement in a heap.

Traffic began to move and Madison laid on the horn once again. This time, the men helped their friend to the shoulder and propped him up against the fence. He wasn't moving.

Madison gunned the accelerator and headed for the shoulder, frightening the two men, who jumped over the fence to safety. Madison had no intention of hurting them. It gave her one more opportunity to teach them a lesson.

Once she cleared the last lamppost, she drove two wheels on the pavement and two wheels on the grassy shoulder. She then roared onto Lynnwood Terrace towards the house.

She looked in the rearview mirror to make sure nobody was following them. Alex looked frantically in all directions as well. They were in the clear, so Madison loosened her grip on the steering wheel.

"You know I was just kidding about the Thelma and Louise thing this morning, right?" asked Alex.

Madison ignored the question and gripped the wheel—doing fifty as she roared past the thirty-mile-per-hour sign on Westview Avenue. After a moment, she calmly asked, "Do you think I killed him?"

She'd lost track of how many laws she had broken that day.

# CHAPTER 35

**5 Hours**
**6:00 p.m., September 8**
**Oval Office, The White House**
**Washington**

If the walls of the Oval Office could talk, the American people would have a much better understanding of how their government worked. A lot happened within the confines of the famous bowed walls designed at the request of President William Howard Taft in the early twentieth century.

Within the confines of the President's personal workspace, domestic and foreign policy was reviewed, advisors were consulted, legislation was signed, and occasionally, events required the President to address the nation via television and radio.

In the two hours prior to the announced address, the President's husband was flown in from Chappaqua on Long Island, the national security team was assembled, and advisors from across the entire governmental and political spectrum were summoned. The President was going to address the nation regarding the impending geomagnetic storm.

The conversations had become contentious several times. The national security and law enforcement advisors insisted upon full disclosure and an announcement of maximum readiness. The political and domestic advisors cautioned against unduly frightening the public, pointing to a mass suicide that occurred in South America earlier in the day by some religious zealots.

A compromise, of sorts, had been reached upon the suggestion of the President's husband. A series of executive orders were drafted and executed by the President in anticipation of a worst-case scenario. The public, however, would be told a watered-down version of the potential impact AR3222 would bestow upon the nation later that evening. Prepare for the worst, without frightening Americans.

The President settled in behind her desk. Flanking her to the viewers' left was the United States flag. To the right stood the official flag of the President of the United States, which consisted of the presidential coat of arms on a dark blue background.

The producers of the event admonished the attendees within the Oval Office to find a seat and quiet down. The President adjusted her suit as she looked into the teleprompter above the camera. She was given the ten-second countdown.

"My fellow Americans, tonight, I address you, and millions of others around the world, regarding a significant space weather event that might affect all of us. There have been a lot of misconceptions bantered about, as well as fearmongering among many in the press and on Capitol Hill.

"Our nation is blessed with some of the most talented scientists and astronomers in the world. Through their efforts over many decades, from the first time we launched a rocket into space until Neil Armstrong uttered those famous words—that's one small step for man, one giant leap for mankind—as he stepped on the lunar surface in 1969, our nation has led the world in space exploration, and monitoring.

"Today, we have been alerted to a significant space weather event emanating from the Sun. I will not delve into the scientific findings and the probabilities at this time. We will be disseminating a summary to the news media, and we ask that the media act responsibly in its reporting.

"Whether this particular solar event will hit the planet directly or deliver a glancing blow is yet to be determined. My staff has prepared a graphic, which is being shown to you at this time, so that you can better understand the basics of solar activity. It is also available on WhiteHouse.gov.

"I will say this, your government is prepared for every possible contingency as this solar flare approaches our planet. For years, contingency plans and continuity of government directives have been in place to protect the American people in times of crises. Today is no exception. We are here to protect you and to do our part in the event of a required recovery operation. But there are things you can do to help us, our first responders, and your neighbors.

"Out of an abundance of precaution, I have declared the entire nation except for Hawaii to be in a state of national emergency. There are several common aspects of what this entails, which I will advise you of now.

"First, stay home. Leave the roads open for first responders to assist those in need. Toward that end, I have instructed the Department of Homeland Security to issue a nationwide curfew of dusk. I urge you to comply with this simple request and be in your homes or another secure location as night comes.

"Second, listen to and comply with the orders of state and local law enforcement. This solar event will impact different parts of the country in different ways. If you don't follow the instructions that apply to your particular part of the nation, you are likely to be injured or find yourself in the way of law enforcement activities.

"Third, as commander in chief, my highest priority is to protect our nation from all threats, foreign and domestic. Toward that end, I have recalled our American troops to American soil for the purposes of assisting law enforcement in the event a recovery effort is necessary. The military's traditional role will be repurposed to assist the Department of Homeland Security in every means necessary to achieve order in the streets of America.

"Fourth, I have executed an executive order that immediately freezes consumer prices across the board. This will apply to everything from hotel rooms to food, gasoline, and essential services. No American should become a profiteer in times of national distress.

"All of us should work together. Share your resources with one another. After you have ensured your own safety, consider the health and welfare of your neighbors. Your government will be there to help you through this potentially trying time.

"Thank you. Godspeed to each and every one of you, and God bless America."

# CHAPTER 36

**4 Hours**
**7:00 p.m., September 8**
**Ryman Residence**
**Nashville, Tennessee**

"No more *runs*, okay, Mom?" Alex laughed as she lifted the rear deck lid and hoisted one of the propane tanks out onto the brick driveway with a clank.

"Oh, I agree," she replied. "This was worth the effort, don't you think?"

"Yeah, and we didn't get in a fight—for a change."

"Sort of," mumbled Madison, wondering if she'd overreacted as the men harassed them.

Madison unconsciously touched her still-swollen cheek as a reminder of their first excursion. She made a mental note to apply copious base makeup before Colton arrived home. He would be worn out from his trip, and she didn't want him to be overly concerned.

"What about the generator?" Alex grabbed the box by the cardboard handle and slid it towards the edge of the bumper. "Never mind. Let Daddy get it. Generators are boy toys anyway." Alex stretched for the bag of guns from Phillips Toy Mart and closed the lid.

As dusk turned to night, the Ryman women arranged everything they had acquired today in the dining room. Their stockpile now encroached into the living area. For the next half hour, Madison roamed around the house, looking for anything useful to add to the pile. She couldn't sit still because Colton now consumed her thoughts. *Where is he? Why hasn't he called?*

She pulled all of the toiletries from the guest bathrooms and stacked them together. She found a Ziploc bag full of complimentary hotel shampoo, conditioner, soaps and sewing kits from a vacation they took to Disney World a year ago. In a guest closet, a pool bag full of ChapSticks, sunscreens, and lotions were left over from the same trip. After mentally chastising herself for not finding a proper storage space for these items, she quickly complimented herself for her forethought.

Madison replayed the conversation she had with Mr. Hart while he helped load up their purchases from the hardware store. He referred to the *Hart Family Trading Post*. Money wouldn't do any good if the power was out for weeks, months or years. Life would be like the old days when a trader would exchange a beaver pelt for a bushel basket of corn.

She immediately turned to the china hutch, where Madison accumulated several bottles of wine and liquor for Friday night's party. The Rymans didn't drink, but most of their neighbors did. She could trade them a bottle of wine for something her family didn't have. *Liquor might be more valuable than hundred dollar bills.*

The china hutch also contained a large selection of pillar and tapered candles. Oddly, this find prompted her to think of insects. She went through the French doors and made her way to the pool house. A helicopter was heard overhead, circling an area towards their west near Belle Meade.

Inside the pool house, she found citronella candles, insect repellents, and a jug of Ortho Max Insect Killer. She picked it up to give it a shake. It was full. *Just because the apocalypse is upon us doesn't mean the bugs run away from our home.* The pool house search also yielded granulated chlorine, which she thought could be useful in purifying water. She made a mental note to look it up in the books she bought. There were also trash bags, some tiki torches with fuel, and a box of fireworks left over from a rain-cancelled July 4th get-together. She carried in the first load and laid the things on the floor near the dining room.

*DING, DONG! DING, DONG!*

Madison jumped at the unexpected, shrieking pitch of the doorbell. Her body immediately was overcome with emotion and then fear. *Is it the police coming to tell her about Colton? Who would be coming by in the dark with all that is going on?*

*KNOCK! KNOCK! KNOCK! KNOCK!*

*Oh no! It's that loud, authoritative pounding of the door that the cops use on television to demand entry.*

"Mom! What should we do?" Alex scrambled on the sofa and immediately pulled the toy Taurus pistol out of the bag. Her hands were shaking, and for the first time, Madison sensed fear in her daughter.

Madison gathered herself and immediately went to the solid, carved wood double doors. She instantly regretted not installing a peephole to see who was on the other side. She carefully pulled the window sheers aside and saw the legs of a woman dressed in seersucker shorts. She let out a sigh of relief. *It isn't the police, and it doesn't appear to be a thug.*

Madison opened the door and greeted her neighbors Shane and Christie Wren. Shane was a political science professor at Vanderbilt University, and Christie was the stay-at-home mother who was riding bikes with her two girls on the sidewalk earlier in the day. He also happened to be the president of the Harding Place Association, a loosely bound group of neighbors who held meetings once a year to talk about things like lawn care standards, improper Christmas displays, and other matters of national importance like parking your cars outside of your garage for extended periods.

"Hi, Shane and Christie," said Madison, peering around the open door. "You guys startled us."

"Oh, we're sorry about that, Madison," said Shane. "As president of the HPA, I thought I would be remiss if I didn't pay our neighbors a visit and discuss current events."

"No, that's okay," said Madison, who still held the door half open. "It's just that, well, you know, it's dark and there's a lot going on today."

"Well, that's part of the reason I wanted to stop by and speak to everyone. There's an abundance of false information out there. All of this doomsday talk is unproductive. Now you know, these solar flares happen all the time."

Madison imperceptibly shook her head. *Go ahead, stick your head in the sand.* She was sure most of the residents comprising the HPA thought like Shane Wren.

"Yeah, you're probably right. Much ado about nothing." Madison attempted a laugh to mask her real beliefs.

Christie was stretching her neck to look past Madison. "It's kind of dark out here."

Madison took the hint and reached across the closed half of the doors and flipped on the foyer and porch lights at the same time. *Big mistake.* The lights illuminated her battered face.

"Oh my gosh, Madison!" exclaimed Christie. "Are you okay, dear? Shane, look at her face."

Shane and Christie both leaned towards Madison to get a closer look, which caused her to recoil abruptly and cover her bruised cheek with her hand.

"Oh, it's nothing," started Madison as she laughed nervously. "You should see the other guy." They weren't laughing with her.

"Madison," started Shane, dragging out the pronunciation of her name, "where's Colton?"

"Um, he's out of town," she replied. "But he should be home anytime. I can have him call you." She closed the door slightly to obstruct their view of the food and supplies in plain view behind her.

The Wrens glanced at each other with that *all-knowing, we've got this situation pegged* look. Christie pointed to the luggage by the foyer closet door.

"Are you guys going on a trip?" she asked.

Madison turned and looked at where she was pointing. Crap! She tried to downplay the luggage. "Oh, no. Not with all that's going on. I mean, you know, Alex and I were cleaning out the closets while we're waiting for Colton to get home."

Alex approached quietly from the living room, her bare feet not making a sound. She leaned into Madison's ear and asked, "Mom, is everything all right?"

"MY GOD," shrieked Christie. "Is that a g-g-gun?" Alex had forgotten to put down the replica handgun.

"Wait, oh, you mean this?" she replied. "This is just a toy we found in the, um, the closet." Alex began to wave the gun around to indicate its harmlessness, which frightened the bejesus out of the Wrens. They immediately jumped back and held up their hands in unison.

Inwardly, Madison laughed at the unintended effect. She thought the conversation was over, but Shane persisted.

"Madison, do you and Alex need some help?" he asked. He pressed on. "Should we call someone, the police perhaps?"

"Why would you call the police?" Madison shot back, trying not to get agitated. "Because of the gun? It's a toy, for Pete's sake. Alex, give that to me so I can show them ..."

Christie was clutching Shane by the arm, pulling him away from the front door. "Honey, let's go," she urged.

"But," started Shane as he also tried to peer past Madison to get a better look inside. Madison stopped any further inquiry.

"Listen, you guys, I was involved in a scuffle at the ATM earlier today. It was nothing more than that. It's late. We're tired. If there's nothing else, I think we should say good night."

"No, of course," replied Shane.

"Are you sure, Madison?" asked Christie. "You and Alex are certainly welcome to come stay with us, you know, for a few days, if you want."

"No, I don't want. Good night!" said Madison as she closed the door and held it shut with her back. She could hear them talking outside.

*Is Colton an abuser?*
*Should we report it?*
*I had no idea.*
*Poor woman.*
*Do you think he beats Alex too?*

Madison was fuming. She wanted to open the door and give them a piece of her mind, but she held back. Her biggest concern was revealing all of her *preps*. *Wait. Preps.* She used the word for the first time as it related to the food and supplies they'd gathered.

*I'm a prepper now.*

# CHAPTER 37

**4 Hours**
**7:20 p.m., September 8**
**T Ricks CITGO, Interstate 40**
**Hazen, Arkansas**

It was getting darker as Colton finally cleared the traffic twenty miles east of Little Rock. Just as the President's address to the nation ended, so did his Sirius satellite feed. He tuned into a local radio station, KARN, and listened to the commentary on the President's handling of the threat. They were not kind to her.

He began to study his fuel gauge and performed some calculations. He might be able to make it to Memphis, which at this pace was only an hour or so away. But he knew enough about the city that pulling off for gas in a Corvette was a death wish. He would start looking for a gas station in one of the small towns between here and Memphis.

Colton turned up the radio as the conversation shifted to the effect of the solar storm on electronics and vehicles. FoxNews was streaming live on KARN now, and Greta Van Susteren was interviewing a professor from MIT.

*"Thank you for having me on, Greta. First, let's establish a few given facts. There hasn't been any credible resource that has conducted testing on the effects of an electromagnetic pulse on a vehicle other than the recent use of the EMP cannon by law enforcement to disable a vehicle. When the high-altitude nuclear testing took place in the 1950s and early 1960s, automobiles did not have the extensive wiring and electronics of today's models."*

*"What about today's vehicles? My car is wired like a rocket ship. How could*

*that possibly survive an EMP?"* asked Van Susteren.

*"It probably would not survive a high-altitude EMP delivered by a nuclear warhead. But it is unlikely that a geomagnetic storm would harm an automobile's electronics because the E3 component of the electromagnetic pulse is not strong enough to cause damage to the wiring."*

*"So our cars will not be affected?"*

*"You'll appreciate this, counselor."* The guest laughed, making an obvious reference to Van Susteren's previous career as an attorney. *"The answer is yes, no, and maybe."*

*"I object!"* interjected Van Susteren.

*"Modern automobiles have as many as one hundred microprocessors that control virtually all functions. Depending on the strength of the electromagnetic pulse, these microprocessors will cease to function. On a scale of one to ten, with ten being the worst-case scenario for this geomagnetic storm, and one being a more typical C-class storm, I'd put the likelihood at a ten that most vehicles will shut down. This geomagnetic storm has the potential to be unlike any other this planet has endured in modern history."*

*"Are you saying we'll be walking everywhere or riding bikes?"*

*"That is the maybe part of your answer. For those lucky few who own an operating vehicle older than 1970, generally considered to be the pre-electronics age in the development of automobiles, you may be in luck."*

*"How so?"* asked Van Susteren.

*"Vehicles from the fifties and sixties will most likely continue to operate,"* he replied.

Colton slowed as he approached a deserted-looking exit for the small town of Hazen, Arkansas. A blue highway sign indicated a couple of fuel options, including a Shell station and a CITGO named T Ricks. Both sides of the interstate had featured fields of soybean and little in the way of residential housing. This might be his best opportunity to fill up and, more importantly, call home.

The Shell station was closed and had been boarded up as if they expected a hurricane. T Ricks logo featured a neon green drawing of a *Tyrannosaurus rex* and appeared to be open. He pulled into the pumps.

Attached to the pump with duct tape was a handwritten sign that read *CASH ONLY, PRICES SUBJECT TO CHANGE.* Colton suddenly wished he was wearing overalls and driving a busted-up truck like those in the parking lot. He imagined the conversation. *Well, sir, for Leon over here, the price is three dollars a gallon. For you,* Mister City Slicker, *today's price is eight hundred and thirteen dollars a gallon.*

Colton didn't have a choice. He exited the Corvette and took the keys with him. There was an eighteen-wheeler parked to the side with its driver standing nearby, smoking a cigarette. A Nissan truck, an old Jeep Wagoneer, and a blue pickup carrying a four-wheeler were parked to the left side of the building. *Here we go.*

Colton pushed open the doors into the convenient store and immediately felt three sets of eyes staring a hole through him. Behind the counter was a large man sporting a rotund belly and a wifebeater shirt. Two other men stood across the store from him, drinking beer. Colton stopped dead in his tracks, not sure of where to start. Finally, after a brief stare-down, he turned his attention to the man behind the counter.

"I need some gas. How much is it a gallon?"

The man stared back and didn't respond.

"Where you from?" asked the tall, lanky beer drinker to his right. Colton didn't want any trouble, but he was extremely nervous at this point. These guys weren't the Welcome Wagon.

"I'm from Nashville," he replied with his best Southern accent.

"That's a pretty car you got there, bud," said the beer drinker's companion after letting out a belch. "Say, you been down on your knees, bud?"

Colton felt panic as a scene from Deliverance flashed through his head. As he saw them staring down at his knees, Colton remembered he'd ripped them open ducking from the gun fire. They were now covered in dried blood.

"Looks like he's either been prayin' or messin' with them boys in Lonoke County!" laughed tall and lanky. This elicited a series of guffaws and bellows from the Hazen boys. Colton didn't like where this was headed and quickly glanced outside to see if any other customers were headed this way. The parking lot and gas pumps were empty except for his Corvette. The driver of the big rig was gone as well.

"Listen, fellas, I'd like to talk some more, but I really need to fill up, pick up a few things, and hit the road. So how much is your gas?"

The big man behind the counter responded, "It's four hundred a fill-up, full service, of course." This brought another roar of laughter from the peanut gallery. Colton was trying to assess whether these three clowns were a threat or simply enjoying themselves at his expense.

"Okay," said Colton. "I saw an ATM sign outside. Where is it?" He looked around and found it for himself. He studied the ATM and learned he could only withdraw two hundred dollars at a time, with a fee of six dollars for each withdrawal. T-Ricks must not have gotten the memo from the President about price-gouging.

"Well, bud, ain't you gonna use it? There ain't no full service on the ATM pump." More roars of laughter as the sound of another sixteen-ounce beer being opened urged Colton to get a move on. Colton made three withdrawals, giving him around eight hundred dollars.

He walked to the cooler and grabbed three bottles of water and two packaged egg salad sandwiches. He found a bag of Munchos potato chips and set the items on the counter. He looked around for a phone car charger. If the circumstances had been different, he would have asked to use the phone. At this point, he just wanted to get the heck out of Dodge, or Hazen, in this case.

"Do you have a car charger for a cell phone?"

The man turned and pulled one off a pegboard rack behind him. An orange sticker revealed a price of twelve dollars. "They're a hundred dollars, today only," he announced. More roars of laughter from his entourage.

"Say, bud," said tall and lanky, walking closer to Colton. Colton glanced outside again, seeking any type of assistance. Still the same three cars and no new patrons. "Whadya say I take your shiny Vette for a little ride after I fill 'er up. I'm tired of drivin' that old Wagoneer. Ya wouldn't mind that, now would ya?"

Colton instinctively backed away from the man, who was getting too close for comfort. He held up both hands and said, "Listen, I just wanna get back to Nashville. Let me pay your friend for the gas and these other things, and I'll get out of your way."

"C'mon, Bubba, leave 'em be," said the man behind the counter.

"Yeah, Otis is right," said Bubba's sidekick. *Bubba and Otis. No surprise there.* Bubba pressed forward.

Colton's survival instincts took over. Every human being was capable of a fight-or-flight reaction when threatened by a potential attack or threat to their survival. Colton's reaction was swift and based on his years of training. His options were to flee, run out the door as fast as he could and find gas elsewhere, or he could fight, which was not his nature, but might be his only option, though not likely to end well.

Or he could negotiate, which was his forte. Colton was always a very quick thinker. During any negotiation, you had to be able to react and seize an opportunity when it presented itself. Colton had a solution.

"Listen, Bubba, I have a deal that you're gonna like," said Colton as he pulled the keys out of his pocket. Bubba stopped and took another swig of beer, followed by a series of belches that came out of his throat like *burpity, burp, burp, burp.*

"Well, bud, I'm in a dealin' frame of mind. Whatcha got?"

Colton began to feel the tension ease out of his body. The boys were on his turf now.

"How 'bout a simple trade? My Corvette for your Jeep Wagoneer. Straight up, and I'll even spend another couple of hundred bucks with Otis on some things for the road."

Bubba started laughing and spilled some of his beer, drawing an admonishment from Otis. "Party foul, brother."

Bubba glanced past Colton and stared at the car. Then he stroked his beard. "Title for title?"

"Well," started Colton. "Yeah, except I don't have the title. I'd have to mail it to you." This brought roars of laughter from everyone.

"Do it, Bubba," said Otis. "You don't need the man's title. Your daddy's sheriff. You could drive around this county with the top off and your pants around your knees without gettin' stopped. Besides, you've been wantin' new wheels for a while now."

"Yeah, Bubba, make the deal!" encouraged his sidekick.

Colton held his breath. Every good closer knew when to shut his mouth. The only movement he made was raising his right arm to show Bubba the key ring with the shiny, stainless Corvette logo engraved on it.

Bubba stared at the car, finished off his beer, let out the obligatory chorus of burps, and said, "Deal!"

# CHAPTER 38

**4 Hours**
**7:45 p.m., September 8**
**Ryman Residence**
**Belle Meade, Tennessee**

Alex continued to monitor the news while Madison completed her rummaging through the pool house. She was still troubled by the visit from the Wrens. They were nosy neighbors and huge gossips. On the surface, their offers of helping others in the HPA would appear admirable. In reality, it was a way for them to brag on their good deeds and stay in everybody's business. Her biggest fear was the spreading of false rumors about Madison's injuries. As she looked back on the conversation, Christie and Shane implied Colton was responsible for the beating.

Suddenly, Alex was yelling for her through the back door. "Mom, are you out here?"

Madison dropped everything and ran onto the pool decking. "Is everything okay?"

"It's Dad! He sent us some texts!"

Madison's heart was racing. She would never admit it, but she was genuinely thrilled, and relieved, that Colton was not hurt or worse. She'd kept busy preparing during the day, but now her thoughts were constantly on Colton.

"What do they say?" she asked, greeting Alex at the French doors. Alex quickly read the series of text messages.

"They must have all come through at once," replied Alex.

C: I'm on my way. Dallas was chaos. Flights x-celed.

C: East of Little Rock now. Had to rent a car. A vette.

C: Traded the vette for a beater truck. Will explain.

C: I miss you guys. Love you more than you know!

Madison began to cry uncontrollably. *He's safe and on his way!* Alex also started crying and hugged her mom. The entire day, they had endured so much yet continued to put on a good front for each other. They were Ryman women and would stay strong for each other. But for the moment, they let it all out.

"See, Mom." Alex laughed, wiping away her tears. "I knew it all along."

"Ha-ha, Alex. Of course you did." Madison grinned and sniffled. She wiped her nose on her sleeve, which was allowed during mother-daughter moments. Alex did the same, which elicited more laughs of relief.

Madison turned her attention to the last of the things she found in the pool house, which included some snacks, cases of soda, and a hammock. Alex quickly helped her, and they locked the door behind them.

"Honey, let's pull all the curtains closed and turn off any unnecessary lights. At night, people can see in, but we can't see out. I thought about that when the Wrens arrived at the front door. I wonder how much they saw?"

"Too much, obvi," replied Alex. "They should mind their own business."

"I agree," said Madison. "How about your daddy renting a Corvette. Do you think he's having a midlife crisis?"

"A what?" asked Alex as she dove back into her laptop.

"Nothing." A siren wailed as two police cars sped down Harding Place towards Belle Meade.

"Holy crap, Mom! Check this out!" shouted Alex.

"What is it?"

"We're famous! Janie just emailed me this. Someone filmed us at the ATM and posted it to YouTube. Well, Channel Five posted it. Check it out!"

Madison closed the last of the living room curtains and turned off the foyer light. She used her toes to kick off her sneakers and ran to join Alex on the sofa. Alex pushed play.

The video started after Madison was initially knocked to the ground. It showed the man trying to wrestle the money away, and the voices of the other ATM customers could be heard in the background.

*"Should we help her?"*

*"I'm not getting out of line."*

*"Oh, look at the girl."*

From the left side of the camera operator's perspective, Alex ran by in a flash, raising the golf club with all her might, which produced a downswing landing squarely in the mugger's ribs. The crack could be heard over the microphone.

"Holy sh…!" exclaimed one of the bystanders as Alex pummelled the man. "Dat girl be kray-kray!"

The video ended with Alex helping her mom to her feet.

"Wow," said Madison, collapsing back into the oversized sofa. "It happened so fast."

"*Kray-kray*," muttered Alex. "I'll show you crazy. I should have grabbed another club and beat all of those people for not helping. Can you believe that, Mom?"

Alex reached for the remote and turned to channel five, WTVF. The news did not replay the attack, but their crews were all over town. The reason for the Belle Meade Boulevard closure was revealed. A woman had been stabbed multiple times in an apparent carjacking. Two men had attacked her and attempted to steal her car. They drove off but lost control on a curve and crashed into a tree. The police were still searching for the two men, but the news reporter indicated that first responders had their hands full and had been unsuccessful in their search.

The news anchor, Carrie Sharp, reported that local law enforcement was unable to enforce the curfew. They were overwhelmed responding to reports of looting and strong-arm robberies. A melee had broken out at a Walmart in North Nashville as a group of teens stormed the sporting goods department. They caught the clerk off guard and performed a smash and grab, stealing guns and ammo. Store security personnel were powerless to stop their escape.

Madison switched the channel to Fox News, which showed scenes of the National Guard moving into place in the nation's capital. Barricades were being established to prevent access to the city. The headlines changed continuously, but indicated the President, the Vice President, and the Cabinet were being moved into undisclosed, secure locations.

Finally, a BBC report showed a video of a group descending upon the French village of Bugarach. A small town in southern France, it was prophesized that Bugarach was the only place to survive an end-of-the-world event. For many years, it was rumored the local mountain—the Pic de Bugarach—held mystical powers. Visitors were known to perform strange rituals, which at times frightened the local population. Now, it had become a perceived place of refuge.

Madison thought about their home and its location. They were surrounded by twenty-five thousand people in their zip code of 37205. If she included the adjacent neighborhoods in 37215, the population doubled to fifty thousand. Within a few square miles! All of those people could become a threat when they became desperate.

What about outsiders? She had never experienced anything like those men attacking their truck today. And a carjacking on Belle Meade Boulevard? That was a first in her dozen or more years of living on Harding Place. Her mind began to race. If this was the reaction of people before the solar flare hit, what would it be like when the power went off? Especially when the nation learned that it wasn't coming on again for a long time.

She got off the sofa and began to wander aimlessly through each room in their home. She went upstairs and approached all of the windows, cautiously looking around the perimeter of their yard. She never thought of where they lived as a place to *hunker down*, as they said on TV shows. Now she was looking at it from a different perspective.

*Is it safe here, a place of refuge?* Belle Meade was known as the wealthiest zip code in Metro Nashville. *Would it be an obvious target for looters and thugs?* She shuddered as she unconsciously shook off the thought.

She wanted Colton home.

# CHAPTER 39

**3 Hours**
**8:15 p.m., September 8**
**Interstate 40**
**West Memphis, Arkansas**

It was pitch dark now, and Colton was concerned about the effect the President's curfew order would have on his ability to pass through Memphis. News reports from major cities were pretty bleak. The country was already slipping into anarchy.

Colton didn't feel one bit guilty for duping Bubba out of his 1969 Jeep Wagoneer. Of course, on the surface, the deal was very one sided. The Vette was probably worth eighty thousand dollars. But he didn't own it. His American Express Gold card would cover the loss to the car rental company, and he might be faced with a hefty credit card bill, if it even mattered after tonight.

His text messages to Madison and Alex gave him newfound resolve despite their lack of response. In his gut, he knew they were safe. It had been a long, stressful day. Seeing the Mississippi river and the lights of Memphis reminded him that he was back where he belonged, even if there were still two hundred miles to go. *I don't care, I could walk from here*, he tried to tell himself.

He had another route decision to make. Interstate 40, to his left, went straight through the heart of Memphis—a dangerous proposition. Although shorter, the city was crime-ridden on a good day. With the reports of chaos nationwide, the inner city was no place to be.

He studied a map he'd bought at T Ricks as he approached the split in the highways. His other choice, a longer route, was to take I-

55 to the south, loop down through northern Mississippi and back up to Jackson via the backroads. He was less likely to encounter rioters and looters, and he didn't think local law enforcement would be setting up roadblocks to enforce the President's curfew. If the cops were smart, they'd be home taking care of their families, as he was trying to do.

Approaching the divided highway, he saw flashing blue lights at the base of the arched Hernando de Soto Bridge, which crossed the Mississippi River into Memphis. The bridge was named after the famed Spanish explorer who navigated up the river in the sixteenth century and died near here. It appeared a roadblock was being established, preventing people from entering the city. He chose the less-traveled Interstate 55 route instead.

The Wagoneer had an AM radio and an under-dash-mounted cassette player. Colton wasn't sure cassettes were even available to purchase anymore except on eBay. Bubba was kind enough to leave Colton with his copy of Lynyrd Skynyrd's greatest hits. It reminded Colton of his father, who grew up on Southern rock and roll. Country music was trending in that direction as well. Country-pop crossovers were the norm rather than the exception now.

Colton glanced at the Memphis airport to his right, and all flights were grounded. Traffic on the interstate was virtually nonexistent. This worried him somewhat because he wanted to fly under the radar now, a big change from his high-flying attitude in the Corvette. He couldn't afford the loss of time resulting from another traffic stop or a government-mandated roadblock.

His trip from DFW had begun as a race against time. Based on the news reports, an ETA of 11:00 p.m. had been established for the arrival of the brunt of the storm. *What if they were wrong on the news about the time of impact?*

He knew it would be close, but he had some comfort in knowing this '69 model Jeep would keep running. Still, in the event it quit, every mile ticked off the highway was a mile he didn't have to walk to get home to his girls.

*Welcome to Mississippi*, the sign read as he drove alone on the eastbound highway. He drove with the windows down, mostly because the air-conditioning didn't work very well and because there was a ghastly smell coming from the back of the Wagoneer. Bubba had either deposited a dead deer, or a decomposing body, in the rear at some point. Regardless, it was awful.

The smell of the gasoline didn't help either. He'd purchased three five-gallon cans and filled them up. Although they didn't leak, the fumes would have proved deadly with his windows rolled up. If the pundits were correct, gasoline would become a valuable commodity after the power grid collapsed.

He would have just enough gas to get home in the twelve-mile-per-gallon behemoth. When it was introduced in 1969, gas prices were thirty-five cents per gallon. Colton's father told stories of competing gas stations having gas price wars. The stations would battle each other for the lowest price at an interchange. Quarter-a-gallon prices were not unusual. But then, OPEC felt it was being cheated and they started squeezing production, gradually quadrupling gas prices. Once prices hit a dollar a gallon, there was no looking back.

Colton's mind was wandering again when he let off the gas pedal, but not because he was speeding. The Wagoneer had a governor on the accelerator, of sorts. As soon as the truck reached seventy miles an hour, the front end would shake uncontrollably because the wheels were out of balance or the front end was out of alignment—or probably both.

He thought about how comfortable life was for Americans. Technology gave them the opportunity to make automobile tires spin at high speeds without vibrations. Computers could be attached to a vehicle's computer and diagnose every aspect of its functionality. Information was at their fingertips via the Internet. They could fly from coast to coast in less than seven hours—a trip that took the early settlers, using a horse-drawn carriage, months.

The experts on the radio warned this one giant burst from the sun would strip those modern conveniences in a given moment. It would change everything. Technologically, it would throw America back into the 1800s.

Colton suddenly became very thankful for his family and the good things he had. He promised himself he would never take them for granted.

# CHAPTER 40

**2 Hours**
**9:00 p.m., September 8**
**Bolivar Highway**
**Jackson, Tennessee**

The barricades crossing Bolivar Highway and the two police cars blocking the road stood in direct contradiction to the sign Colton was parked next to, which read *Jackson Welcomes You, We're Glad You're Here*. This was clearly not a welcoming committee.

He turned off the truck and took out the small LED flashlight he'd purchased at T Ricks. He turned the page in the *Rand McNally Road Atlas* and studied his alternatives. He was immediately upset with himself. He should have studied back-road options before getting in this predicament.

About fifteen minutes ago, he'd crossed Highway 100, which would take him directly to Nashville. There were dozens of small towns in between, any of which could pose a roadblock problem or potential looters, but at least it was progress. With no viable options around the city of Jackson, Colton closed up the map and turned around. He found the first side street headed east and made his way through the neighborhoods.

It was an odd sight. People were talking in their front yards, some cooking on their grills. In some respects, it resembled a Fourth of July block party. Many of the men were carrying rifles slung over their shoulders. As he drove by, he garnered their attention. None of the residents made a threatening move toward him, but he was clearly being watched.

As he turned south on US 45 and made his way back to Highway

100, he thought about his neighbors. Their home was not conducive to neighborhood social interaction. The houses were spread apart with long driveways to a private garage area. Although Harding Place had a sidewalk to encourage walking, jogging, and bike riding, the road itself was heavily traveled as an east-west route from Belle Meade to Interstate 65 and beyond to the Nashville airport. As a result, the types of block parties Colton just observed didn't exist. They rarely held get-togethers with their neighbors. Even Friday night's soiree would be made up of primarily business acquaintances, with the exception of a couple of neighbors.

Colton easily passed through the small town of Henderson and sped up Highway 100. He felt he was on the home stretch. He looked at the inexpensive Timex Camper watch he'd purchased from T Ricks for its actual retail price of thirty-five dollars. He thought it would be handy if the solar storm ruined his Apple watch, which would be worthless in any event.

It was just after 9:00. Colton tried to call home. *All circuits are busy.* The phone was fully charged now, but he kept it plugged in. From what he heard on the radio, the phone would be fried anyway, but he thought he'd keep it charged just in case it wasn't. He tried a text message. It left his phone with a *swoosh.*

C: *East of Jackson. Love you guys!*

Colton held the phone for several minutes, anticipating a response. It never came. Colton was unaware that text would never go through.

As he drove northeast toward the small town of Decaturville, he tried to reach Madison several times but the *all circuits are busy* recording was working overtime. He was within hours of home, but the brunt of the solar flare was already bearing down on the planet.

It was dark on this deserted stretch of highway as he passed towns like Jack's Creek and Lick Skillet. The fertile lowland of the Tennessee River basin in West Tennessee was prime real estate for growing cotton, soybeans, and other crops. Colton leaned forward in his seat and looked up at the sky. It was beginning to exhibit the early aurora effect as promised by the weather watchers.

The bright dancing lights of the electrically charged particles from the sun were created as they entered the earth's atmosphere. At this point, the faint colors of blue and green engulfed the sky in a thin cloud or veil. The full moon began to rise over the eastern horizon and took on psychedelic colors as its reflection mixed with the hues of blue and green.

Colton wondered how something so beautiful could be so potentially deadly. Then he came to a realization. It wasn't the sun's particles and the beautiful aurora it produced that were going to be deadly. It would be man's reaction to the aftermath—just like his granddaddy said.

*Never underestimate the depravity of man.*

He pressed down on the gas despite the shaking of the front end. He didn't care if the truck shook out all of his fillings. He needed to protect Madison and Alex.

# CHAPTER 41

**Zero Hour**
**11:00 p.m., September 8**
**Ryman Residence**
**Nashville, Tennessee**

The solemn CNN news team of Wolf Blitzer, Jake Tapper, and Don Lemon continued their commentary as their Countdown to Impact Clock approached 0:00—*Zero Hour.* The scene at Times Square in New York was reminiscent of a New Year's Eve countdown without the revelry and deprivation.

The satellite newsfeed became erratic. DirecTV would frequently become frozen and pixelated, as if a serious thunderstorm was passing over Nashville. *Error Code 771* would appear frequently, and then the programming would continue. The World Wide Web had ceased to function consistently about an hour ago as power outages affected web servers around the world.

Madison wrapped all of their small electronic devices in heavy-duty aluminum foil. Then she placed their cell phones, laptops, and portable radios in the cardboard-lined galvanized trash cans purchased at the hardware store. She explained to Alex what she read about Faraday cages. The plan was to shield the electronics from the massive burst of energy created by the solar storm.

They sat on the sofa, held hands, and prayed together—something Madison and Alex hadn't done as mother and daughter for years. They were anxious. Alex kept reminding her mom that the clock was arbitrary. The sun didn't send a memo to the stupid news networks announcing the arrival time of the solar flare. Yet the Impact Clock ticked toward zero anyway.

*Where is Colton?* The Impact Clock was winding down. Under three minutes. Earlier, Madison stopped looking out of the windows after Alex got annoyed. She had been up and down off the sofa constantly for an hour.

Their eyes were fixated on the television monitors. The eyes of the crowd in Time Square were glued to the digital screens and billboards all around the most famous stretch of cityscape in the world—the intersection of Broadway and Seventh Avenue. What had once been dubbed *The Center of the Universe* became a mass of humanity— waiting, hopeful, and full of apprehension.

As the Impact Clock hit 2:22, the bolt lock on the kitchen door snapped. Then the door handle wiggled before the door flung open.

Frightened, Madison jumped and quickly turned to look toward the kitchen.

"Did you miss me?"

She flung herself off the couch and ran around the furniture in that direction. Alex hopped over the back and hit the wood floor in a sprint.

The impact of the two hugging Colton knocked him against the kitchen island. All three of the Rymans were sobbing, holding each other tight, eyes clenched shut. Words were not spoken, but ample tears streamed down everyone's faces.

"I love you guys so much!" Colton managed to say through his sniffles.

"We love you, Daddy!"

"Colton, you have no idea how much we need you. I never want us to be apart again!" said Madison as she buried her face in his chest.

After a moment, Madison pulled away and looked down to hide her bruised face. The attempt to cover bruises and scabs with makeup was erased by the tearful outburst.

"What happened to your knees?" she asked through her sobs as she examined his bloodstained, torn suit pants.

"I hit the pavement and had to scramble away when the gunfire started," he replied.

"Real gunshots?" asked Alex, through the tears.

Colton took his hands and gently lifted Madison's face up to kiss her. He saw her bruises and scrapes. "Oh, honey, what happened?"

"I'm okay," replied Madison. "I got mugged at the ATM today."

"What? Are you hurt elsewhere? Thank God you're okay."

"I beat him with a golf club, Daddy," Alex proudly added.

"Which one?"

"Which one what?" Alex began to ask and then answered her own question, "My sand wedge."

"Good club choice, sweetheart," replied Colton as the laughter helped ease the tension, and the tears. "Thank God you're both okay."

They began to move into the living room when Alex exclaimed, "Hey, look! The clock stopped at zero and nothing happened."

The CNN cameras panned the mass of humanity as a spontaneous eruption of joy and relief filled the packed crowd. The trio of news anchors couldn't contain themselves as they exchanged hugs and handshakes. Jubilation accompanied pandemonium in Times Square, the so-called Center of the Universe, as the bright neon lights from the McDonald's logo to the Bank of America sign continued their dazzling display. Then—

*CRACKLE! SIZZLE! SNAP—SNAP—SNAP!*

Darkness. Blackout.

*Zero Hour.*

Thanks for reading *36 HOURS*, the first book in *The Blackout Series*!

**The saga will continue in…**
**ZERO HOUR**
**Book two of The Blackout Series**

SIGN UP to Bobby Akart's mailing list to receive free advance reading copies, special offers, and bonus content. You'll also be one of the first to receive news about new releases in The Pandemic Series, The Blackout Series, The Boston Brahmin Series and the Prepping for Tomorrow series—which includes sixteen Amazon #1 Bestsellers in 39 different genres.

Visit Bobby Akart's website for informative blog entries on preparedness, writing and his latest contribution to the American Preppers Network.

www.BobbyAkart.com

**Continue reading** for **FREE bonus chapters** from the Amazon #1 Best Seller, **PANDEMIC: BEGINNINGS**.

Best Selling Author of The Blackout Series

# BOBBY AKART

# THE PANDEMIC SERIES ❦ BOOK ONE

Free Bonus Chapters from *PANDEMIC: BEGINNINGS*

# PROLOGUE

*You are free to make your choices, but you are not free to choose the consequences.*

## Western Africa

They were dragging Dr. Francois Alexis through a dark, dusty hallway. He'd become confused at how long he'd been held in the tiny cell, without light, and no sustenance. For days, he'd been bound and gagged. A dark hood was pulled over his head, which also made it difficult to breathe. Dr. Alexis had become completely disoriented in a world of blackness and terror.

Between the beatings and the fitful attempts at sleep, Dr. Alexis was unable to determine whether he'd been held captive for two days or ten. Many events were impossible for him to discern in this starved, sleep-deprived state. *What do they want from me?*

All he could remember was leaving the International Medical Research Centre in the former French colony of Gabon on the West Africa coast late Friday night. He stopped to pick up a sandwich and was hit in the back of the neck with a powerful blow, forcing him to the ground. He remembered the black hood being pulled over his head and he was whisked away in a vehicle to an unknown destination. His attackers never uttered a word throughout the abduction.

The Center for International Medical Research where he worked, known as the CIRMF, was staffed by one hundred sixty-seven scientists and had an annual budget of over five million dollars. Based in Franceville, a city of one hundred thousand in southeast Gabon, the facility boasted a biological research infrastructure, which was rare in Africa, including a biosafety level 4 laboratory. A BSL-4 represented the highest level of biosafety precautions and was designed for working with the world's most dangerous pathogens.

Dr. Alexis was one of a dozen scientists focused on emerging infectious diseases like Ebola, Marburg, and the three varieties of plague. The facility's primatology center was among the largest in the world. Containing five hundred primates, half of which were housed in a jungle enclosure, the CIRMF was ideally suited for testing and researching viruses in their natural hosts.

With his mind racing, seeking answers as well as anticipating what was happening, Dr. Alexis struggled against his captors while peering through the bottom of the black hood, which continued to obstruct his vision.

The more he struggled, the harsher he was treated. When the hood was removed, enabling him to see the floor, he stopped his resistance.

He was forced through an entryway into a brightly lit room, where a variety of power cords and cables spread across the floor. One of his captors yelled at him in Arabic and pushed him into a nondescript wooden chair in the center of the room.

Another man issued orders, barking the words in a guttural language he couldn't interpret, and the room lit up with artificial light, causing Dr. Alexis to wince despite his limited vision. He adjusted his posture in the chair and two strong arms pulled him upright in the chair. Then his hands were strapped to the back of the chair with zip-ties. His legs were bound in a similar manner, which effectively immobilized him. He'd become one with the chair.

The room became eerily silent. There was no speaking. No shuffling of feet. Only the faint sound of an internal fan on a computer or other electronic device, which whirred in the background. The anticipation added to Dr. Alexis's anxiety. His heart was pounding in his chest. He tried to speak, but the gag prevented the words from coming out. *What is happening?*

*ZING!*

The screeching sound of metal on metal filled the room. The noise was familiar, but Dr. Alexis couldn't place it in his agitated state of mind. Horror overtook him as he frantically looked from side to side to locate the source of the sound.

Suddenly, an arm wrapped itself around his forehead and pulled his head back, exposing the pulsating veins in his neck. The young Frenchman felt the cold steel of the blade press against his flesh. He looked down past his nose to catch a glimpse of the weapon. It was a sword, polished chrome glimmering in the light of the room.

He attempted to voice his protest, but that caused his neck to swell and press closer to the sharp blade. His captor let out a throaty laugh, harsh and raspy, which caused the blade to move from side to side ever so slightly.

As if in the hands of a surgeon, the sharp blade pierced his skin, slicing slowly across his neck. His captor's precision was remarkable—not too deep, but enough to produce the desired effect. Warm blood trickled slowly out of the wound, marring the finish on the sword and dripping down onto his partially exposed chest.

*I'm going to die today*, Dr. Alexis convinced himself as he closed his eyes. *I'm about to become the lead news story on France's TF-1.*

His mind raced to his beautiful wife and two young daughters. Josephine had encouraged him to take this job. His pay was doubled because he was away from home, but she thought it would help them provide for their young family. She'd remained behind in Paris while their darling preteen girls went to the finest schools his salary could afford.

They never were concerned about the risks of his working abroad. Gabon was predominantly French and the city of Lawrenceville was relatively crime-free. The biggest concern for Dr. Alexis was mishandling one of the infectious diseases while working in the laboratory. The facility had a spotless accident record and Dr. Alexis was meticulous in his precautionary measures. He was only six months away from returning to Paris with a powerful reference on his résumé.

The blade pressed closer to his neck, opening the wound a little further and drawing more blood. In English, a man instructed his associates to turn on the camera. *This is it*, thought Dr. Alexis. He closed his eyes and apologized to his wife and children. Then he prayed to God to protect his family and forgive him for his sins.

Without warning, more lights were turned on, momentarily blinding him again. His head was snapped backwards and the blade dug into his throat a little bit more. He clenched his eyes shut this time and braced for the impact that would end his life.

The voice of his captor hissed into his ear, "You will only die today, Dr. Alexis, by your own choice. Now open your eyes!"

\*\*\*\*\*

"Where am I?" asked Dr. Alexis as he struggled to find the words and regain his vision. He wasn't sure if he was allowed to speak, but he tried nonetheless.

A fist full of hair caused his head to instantly jerk back, once again stretching his neck and bearing its vulnerability to the blade. This time a sword wasn't the weapon of choice to inflict pain upon him, a cup of salt did the trick. Dr. Alexis screamed out loud as the stinging pain from the table salt met the open wound on his throat. Tears ran down his face. He had never experienced pain like this, much less the brutality of his captors.

"Pay attention, Dr. Alexis," whispered the man behind him while he forced the Frenchman's head to look at the fifteen television monitors mounted on the wall. Only one monitor was on, and it was streaming images of the front of his home in suburban Paris.

Dr. Alexis stared in shock as the single monitor played surveillance video of his house. "What? That is my home! Why are you filming my home?" he shouted at his captor and attempted to wriggle out of his restraints.

A heavy hand covered in salt immediately began to choke his throat, causing him to scream in agony. The man gruffly rubbed his rough hand to grind the salt into the wound. He calmly spoke into Dr. Alexis's ear. "You will not speak until it is time. Do you understand? My next method of pain will be far worse."

183

Dr. Alexis managed a nod but was unable to vocalize the word *yes*. His throat was incredibly dry from fear.

"Turn them all on," instructed the faceless man, who continued to stand behind him. He gripped the doctor's head in both his hands and firmly turned his attention to all the screens.

"Oh no," moaned Dr. Alexis.

"Do you see, Doctor?" the man whispered in his ear. "Do you see your wife and children as we do?"

Dr. Alexis shook his head as tears streamed down his face. He began to sob as the videos were played on all fifteen screens. His children were walking into school together. His wife, naked, was entering the shower. All three girls were watching television. Every aspect of his family's life was played out in front of him.

Dr. Alexis's chin dropped to his chest, despite the searing pain from the wound. He gasped for air as he tried to speak. In Arabic, his captor asked for the pitcher of water sitting on the table to their right. He grasped his captive by the hair and poured water over his head, down his throat, and over his wounded neck. Dr. Alexis coughed violently in an attempt to clear his airway.

"Why? What do you want from me?" he begged.

"It is very simple for a man of your intelligence and position," came the reply. "You are going to do your job in Franceville, but now, you will take your instructions from me. But remember, we will be watching you, and them."

*****

Gabon, where the BSL-4 laboratory in which Dr. Alexis worked was located, was not exactly a hotbed of terrorist activity. Unlike Northern Africa, which was predominantly Muslim, Gabon's population was largely Christian and only five percent of the population was Sunni Muslim.

In the nearby country of the Democratic Republic of the Congo, formerly called Zaire, Islamic State terrorists had created a stronghold as it continued to expand its presence around the world.

Unbeknownst to Dr. Alexis, the DR Congo arm of ISIS was designed for this specific operation.

In the aftermath of the abduction and the revelation that his family was in grave danger, Dr. Alexis considered his options. He feared his movements were so closely tracked that unthinkable harm would come to his wife and young daughters. He became a recluse out of fear of saying or doing something that might be misconstrued by his handlers. He'd focus on the assigned task, and then as soon as practicable, he'd rush to Paris, gather up his family, and head for the Alps to hide.

As instructed, Dr. Alexis positioned himself to work with the team assigned to a recent outbreak of plague in Madagascar. Two of the districts in Madagascar had been declared by the WHO, the World Health Organization, as endemic for the plague bacteria. The most recent outbreak was blamed for sixty-two cases resulting in a fatality rate of eighty-five percent.

Dr. Alexis could not grasp how his ISIS captors came by this information, but their intelligence was correct. The strain of plague that Dr. Alexis was to work with was the deadliest form of the plague known as pneumonic plague, not its more recognizable sister, bubonic plague.

For weeks, he performed his duties in isolation, despite the fact that he was part of a larger research team. He'd become gloomy and unsociable. His co-workers didn't want to associate with him. He maintained limited contact with his family to mask his troubles. He was singularly focused on one thing—complying with his handler's directives.

By analyzing case studies of the dead, Dr. Alexis determined that the Madagascar strain of *Yersinia pestis*, or *Y. pestis* for short, the bacterium causing plague, could be *improved—enhanced.*

His handler's directives were crystal clear, but the choices he had to make were clouded by the love for his family. The moral fight raged within him. There was no one to talk to. The choice was his to make.

Plague was one of the oldest diseases known to humans and had caused over two hundred million deaths worldwide. There was no preventive vaccine. The plague could be treated. However, if it was modified and weaponized...

Sixty days later...

# PART ONE

# WEEK ONE

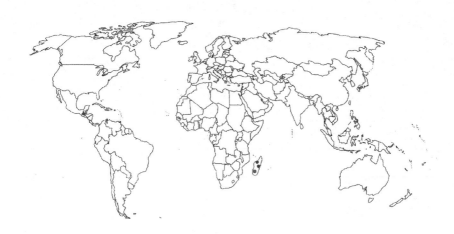

# CHAPTER 1

**Day One**
**Guatemala Jungle near El Naranjo**

"It's too early in the morning for interviewing dead people," mumbled Dr. Mackenzie Hagan as she sloshed her way through the wet jungle path, which was well worn at this point from activity. She attempted to duck under the low-lying branches of a thorny lime tree and was almost successful before it grabbed her ponytail, which protruded through the strap of her cap.

She had taken a hodgepodge of modern transportation from Atlanta overnight, bouncing from a packed-like-sardines Delta flight, to a single-wing Cessna, and finally a decades-old Jeep J8 Patrol Truck, which was utilized by the Guatemalan military for its *special guests*. With only six percent of the Guatemalan population owning a vehicle, she felt lucky that her options weren't more unconventional. She had only wished the soldier escorting her to the site would keep his eyes on the road and quit trying to sneak a peek down her blouse.

June was one of the wettest months of the year in Guatemala, and this particular day did not buck the norm. A heavy downpour had just ended as the sun began to rise, causing the plant life to wake up in all its glory and the humidity to kick into high gear.

Mac, as her friends called her, was not an early riser. She often joked she either needed twelve hours' sleep or just four hours', although the latter generally resulted in a socially challenged epidemiologist.

After they arrived, Mac stepped out of the Jeep into the wet, soggy jungle. The sounds of chattering monkeys filled the air, as well as a light sprinkle dropping through the tropical foliage. The soldier led the way up a well-worn path created by foot traffic and hand carts carrying the CDC's gear.

Her escort pushed back an areca palm and opened up a gateway to a clearing that stood in contrast to the third-world vistas that made up the northern part of the country. Her counterparts from the Centers for Disease Control and Prevention, the CDC's Central American Regional Office in Guatemala City, had arrived twenty-four hours prior.

White tents surrounded the village, which was nestled into the eastern edge of the Laguna del Tigre National Park on the country's northern border with Mexico. A score of native settlements, dwarfed by the rising hills, lay scattered throughout the jungles of this region, which used to play an important political and economic role in the ancient Mayan world.

Like the nearly two million Indians that made up half of Guatemala's population, the residents of these outlying areas spoke various dialects of the Maya-Quiche language, which evolved from the descendants of the Maya Empire. On this day, as Mac interviewed the dead, the language barrier wouldn't be a factor.

Mac caught her first glimpse of the dead wrapped in colorful body bags and lying unceremoniously on the soggy ground. Signs of village life still remained—tools to cultivate corn and primitive back-strap looms used to create colorful and complex textiles designed to differentiate the village from others nearby.

This village was small by comparison. Only twenty to thirty small adobe houses were compactly grouped around the central square— where most of the bodies lay.

No roads connected this village with others in the jungle. The inhabitants traveled on foot and occasionally on horseback, along narrow paths that wound around precipitous hillsides. They owned no vehicles except for the hollowed-out canoes fortified on each side by clapboards. Mac could visualize a canoe's occupants paddling from a standing position, the one in the stern expertly steering the vessel along nearby Santa Amelia lake.

*What is wrong with me?* She never got distracted on an investigation as serious as this one. Perhaps it was the juxtaposition of a village set in an era a thousand years ago, but now surrounded by modern technological advances. Or it was the sadness of an entire group of people—families, with children, lying dead in their primitive village.

She took a calming breath. She seriously needed to buckle down. Taking her eye off the ball in a situation like this would not be prudent. She let out a tense breath and closed her eyes for a moment.

Mac bit her lip as she studied the scene again, taking into her imagination what life looked like in this desolate village before death came knocking. Several large raindrops snapped her out of her daze as well as the smell of something familiar.

# CHAPTER 2

**Day One**
**Guatemala Jungle near El Naranjo**

"Dr. Hagan, I presume?" asked a lanky technician with a British accent. He extended his arm to shake hands with Mac, who opted instead to adjust her white cap with the letters CDC embroidered in blue across the front. She had abandoned the custom of shaking hands with others years ago. She had seen too much.

"Good morning, Sherlock." Mac chuckled, attempting to bring herself to the land of the living. "Please tell me that's coffee."

"Indeed, ma'am," replied Lawrence Brown, one of the career epidemiology field officers, or CEFOs, stationed in Guatemala City. "A little bird told me that you liked it black, full strength, and piping hot."

"A little bird?" Mac asked, tipping the warm brew into her mouth. She instantly received a waking jolt of energy.

"Tweet, tweet, Mac!" announced a female voice from behind her. Mac turned to view a friendly face. It was one of the EIS officers from Atlanta, Janelle Turnbull, a former veterinarian whom Mac had worked with in the past.

Created in 1951 during the Korean War, the Epidemic Intelligence Service was a postgraduate program established for health care professionals, physicians, and veterinarians interested in epidemiology. Both during and after their course work, these highly qualified individuals would study infectious diseases, environmental health issues, and other tasks within the purview of the CDC. Acceptance to the program was an honor that all of the nearly two hundred participants took seriously. Mac knew Janie to be a tireless worker and willing to travel to any part of the planet to perform her disease-detective skills.

Mac instantly beamed. "Janie, did you catch the wrong MARTA train?"

"No, the muckety-mucks wanted to make sure you had everything you needed down here," replied the petite brunette clad in a newly designed, military-grade biological suit created after the West Africa Ebola crisis. The suit used several zippers and fasteners to fall off and peel outward from the wearer, alleviating the need to touch any outer surfaces.

Prior to this new innovation created by a design challenge launched by the United States Agency for International Development, USAID, the EIS disease detectives would suit up with many layers of gear that took a partner and twenty minutes to dress. Even worn properly, the headgear didn't attach to the body suit, creating an opportunity for a miniscule virus one-billionth our size to slip into the suit.

In addition, the new suit featured an internal cooling system ideally suited for hot climates such as Africa and Guatemala. Air was constantly funneled to the headgear through an air chamber, which helped keep the brain cool. Cooler heads prevented heatstrokes and panic attacks.

"Are you about to go in?" asked Mac. She glanced around to observe the level of activity at this early hour. She also looked to the sky to gauge the possibility of more precipitation. This hot zone had the potential to be a hot mess if it rained much more.

"Yes, but I'd like to bring you up to speed first," Janie replied. "We can go in together after that. Come into the field ops tent. We'll get you dried off and then outfitted in your very own space suit."

Mac followed Janie into a large white tent, which contained an air-locked entry on both ends. The logistics involved in this type of investigation required preplanning and experienced technicians. When dealing with an unknown outbreak, mistakes could be deadly.

Mac got settled in after exchanging pleasantries with some of the field officers from CDC-Guatemala City. Janie quickly returned in her civvies with another cup of coffee for both of them. Disease detectives were very much like their law enforcement counterparts. Coffee fueled their day.

Janie settled in a chair next to Mac and opened a file folder, which contained several thick reports. Mac thumbed through the pages of reports as Janie spoke.

"I'll recap what you probably already know and then tell you what's transpired over the last twenty-four hours," started Janie, taking another sip of coffee before getting down to business. "Four days ago, a young man from another village came here on horseback with a load of yarn to trade. He found all of the villagers to be ill. He described them as being nauseated, weak, and with a high fever."

"How were we notified?"

"He returned to his village to give an account of what he'd seen. One of the village elders traveled into town to report the incident. According to the interview he gave a health care worker from the local hospital in El Naranjo, there were no deaths at the time. The local police and a nurse arrived here two days later. The entire village was dead."

Mac reached for the file full of reports and studied the findings. Eighty-one bodies were found throughout the village. There was evidence of vomiting and bleeding from the mouth.

"We need to conduct autopsies as soon as possible," said Mac. She rubbed her temple as she contemplated the magnitude of the situation. An entire village of eighty people, exhibiting flu-like symptoms, was dead within days.

"That's part of the update," added Janie. "Before we could mobilize and arrive on the scene, half a dozen bodies were removed to the hospital in El Naranjo. The local authorities took them early yesterday morning."

"Are you kidding me? They're not set up for something like this!"

"I know, Mac. I wish I had been here. We got it together pretty fast, but you know how these hot zones are. There's protocol. We've got to protect our own first."

Brown approached the two of them. Janie addressed him first.

"Well, Sir Lawrence, what say you?"

"We're gathering specimens now," he replied. "The good news is that the weather radar indicates this low-pressure system has moved past us. The hot zone won't be further compromised by rainfall. The bad news is that despite the fact the village is small by comparison to American towns, it's big enough that it can't be completely contained."

"Surely to God we can keep onlookers out of the zone," barked Mac. While containment was not within her scope of responsibility, she didn't want to be bumping into looky-loos while she assessed the scene.

"No, ma'am. The problem isn't people, it's the spider monkeys. The jungle is full of them. The military tells us that the village was crawling with them when they first arrived. By nature, the monkeys are scavengers. In addition to being overly curious, they're also looking for food."

"Food that might carry the disease!" Mac raised her voice, drawing the attention of technicians throughout the tent. She took a deep breath to calm down her anxiety. At the same time, as if on cue, the HEPA air filtration for the tent kicked on, causing the walls to quickly expand and then deflate as stale air was forced out to make way for fresh, filtered air.

"We've asked the military to help, but there aren't enough assigned to our location and the ones that are don't want to come anywhere within the outer perimeter of the village," replied Brown. "They're afraid of getting too close."

Janie, who was fluent in Spanish, added, "They're calling the village *Cerro de Muerte*—the Hill of Death."

Mac thought of her escort who'd led her up the path earlier. As soon as they reached the clearing, he'd stopped and left. *He didn't want any part of this detail.*

She contemplated for a moment and then gave Lawrence instructions. "Is there any place to land a chopper up here?" The village was in the midst of dense jungle vegetation. Mac hadn't seen a clearing.

"I'll find out or send someone to locate an opening," replied Brown. "Do you want me to take the bodies to Guatemala City? I'll need to get approval from their government for that."

"Why wouldn't they approve?" asked Mac. "They called us in, right?"

"True, but they assumed we would deal with the investigation here. They're in the midst of a presidential campaign. President Morales would like to see this kept out of the media. In fact, my understanding is that the military will raze the village, together with the bodies, as soon as we're done here."

Mac considered her alternatives. Transporting dead bodies carrying an infectious disease was a dangerous proposition, as she and others had learned during the Ebola outbreak in Guinea, Liberia, and Sierra Leone. Containment was a challenge anyway, but tribal burial customs, which included a final kiss of the deceased loved ones, had assisted in the transmission of the Ebola virus throughout the West Africa region.

After the first cases of Ebola were reported in Guinea in 2013, containment practices were instituted by the World Health Organization, which published a road map of steps to prevent further transmission. These steps were not always followed, and within a year, Ebola had exploded. Mac was not interested in a repeat of those failures.

The nearest U.S. military base was in El Salvador, which was too far away to ferry dead bodies by helicopter. There weren't any good options. She gulped down the last of her coffee and stood, ready to examine some of the bodies for herself.

"Well, we'd better get to work. But, Lawrence—" she paused briefly before continuing "—keep the monkeys out of the village. We don't need this disease spread all over the country."

# CHAPTER 3

**Day One**
**Guatemala Jungle near El Naranjo**

At five foot ten, Mac was accustomed to donning protective gear designed for men. Her slender, athletic build was part genetics, part training. She found working out and participating in athletic events to be an excellent way to relieve stress. Daily, she faced the possibilities of a global pandemic. Some people feared nuclear war or economic collapse. Mac lost sleep over the myriad of possibilities that would result in a large number of deaths like those lying at her feet, multiplied by millions.

Mac had seen the worst of the worst. She had been to Zimbabwe in Southern Africa to investigate an outbreak of Lassa, a viral hemorrhagic fever first identified in Nigeria decades earlier, but had never been seen outside of West Africa. The natives were exhibiting symptoms common to most diseases—high fevers, severe diarrhea, vomiting, and rashes.

The first investigators on the scene from the World Health Organization made a diagnosis of Marburg disease, commonly known as the green monkey disease. Under the microscope, Marburg was distinctive with its long snakelike loops and twists. Lassa was similar in look, but different in treatments. Mac was able to lead researchers at the WHO to a different diagnosis, ultimately saving a lot of lives.

From that experience and others, Mac never accepted an initial hypothesis. She was known to check and recheck specimens. Her personality suited long hours in the lab, avoiding social interaction with co-workers or potential suitors. Mac had no use for the dating game. She enjoyed a quiet evening at home with a cold beer and a science journal.

Janie took Mac on a brief tour of the village to allow the entire picture to come into focus. As specimen gatherers knelt over bodies, carefully extracting tissue and blood samples, Mac would pause to observe.

She approached one of the technicians. "Have you seen any signs of lesions, pustules, or discolored skin tissue?"

"No, ma'am," he replied.

Mac nodded and left the man to his work. She continued her walk with Janie, periodically looking into the small adobe homes. The mostly rectangular structures consisted of block walls, thatched roofs, and only a few rooms. Bodies were found in beds or at times near makeshift latrines behind the homes.

She stopped for a moment and looked toward the perimeter, where two soldiers were jousting with a group of spider monkeys who were attempting to get into the village. "Have you found any dead animals in the village? You know, monkeys, rats, bats, etcetera?"

"Only a dairy cow that was still tied to its post near a barn. The horses, which were kept in a small barn up the hill, were unaffected."

"Have you seen any fleas since you arrived on the scene?"

"No. No mosquitos either. All of the typical carriers of disease appear to be absent except for the monkeys."

Mac motioned for Brown to join them. "Sir Lawrence," started Mac jokingly, "will you coordinate with our soldier friends to capture half a dozen monkeys for analysis? Also, we're gonna need to send our teams out to the surrounding areas to interview anyone who has come in contact with this village."

"I'm already on it," he replied. "Well, one more thing. I want to question the boy who reported the illness. He may be able to shed some light on the condition of the villagers before they died. Sadly, he might also be infected."

Brown hustled off, so Mac and Janie continued. "Why wouldn't they go for help?" queried Mac aloud.

"They just don't believe in modern medicine," replied Janie. "They have their own forms of homeopathic treatments, which obviously didn't work in this case."

"I've spent a considerable amount of time in Africa," started Mac. "Those of us who live in the modern world wouldn't believe that primitive people like this still exist. Despite what happened here, it does prove that mankind can exist without the conveniences of smartphones and fast food."

The two spent another hour surveying each body and discussing the initial findings with members of the CDC team. Brown secured more troops from the Guatemalan military and they were winning the battle in repelling the curious monkey population.

After completing their decontamination process, Mac and Janie returned to their civilian clothes and entered the administration tent to compare notes. As they entered the tent, a man was standing over the shoulder of a microbiologist while studying the file that Janie had provided Mac earlier.

Mac immediately approached the man and firmly snatched the file from his grasp. "May I help you?"

"Well, actually," he started as he removed his Ray-Ban Aviators from his head and tucked them into one of the pockets of his khaki cargo pants, "I was doing just fine until you rudely snatched the file out of my hands."

"Now, hold on, mister," protested Janie. "This file is not for public viewing. Maybe you should identify yourself."

"Sure, Nathan Hunter, Defense Threat Reduction Agency."

"Wait," interjected Mac. "DOD? Why would the Department of Defense be interested in this?"

He didn't respond, but instead stuck out his hand to shake. "And you are?"

As always, Mac avoided shaking hands, drawing a puzzled look from Hunter. "My name is Dr. Mackenzie Hagan with the CDC. This is my associate Janie Turnbull. Now, why are you here?"

Hunter acted sincere and apologetic. "I'm sorry, Miss, um, Dr. Hagan, if I've overstepped my boundary. I'm a soldier, of sorts, so I follow orders. Someone at Fort Belvoir thought it necessary for me to visit, so I'm visiting."

"How about some credentials," said Janie bluntly. Hunter glared down at her for a second before reaching into his shirt pocket and producing an ID issued by the Defense Threat Reduction Agency.

Janie handed it to Mac, who returned the laminated ID card to Hunter. Because of her mother's background, Mac was familiar with the DTRA, which was an agency within the DOD. Their main function was countering weapons of mass destruction, which included chemical, biological, and nuclear threats.

Hunter continued to focus on Mac, who was momentarily mesmerized by his steel-blue eyes. The man was an intruder into her realm, but he was handsome and built like he was carved out of granite. She seriously doubted this Mr. Hunter's sole responsibility with the DTRA was bird-dogging an isolated disease outbreak.

"Seriously, I don't want to get in your way," said Hunter. "I happened to be in the region and was asked to stop by to get an update. My superiors are interested in this sort of thing."

"Well, Mr. Hunter, *this sort of thing* can have catastrophic consequences just as much as Assad's chemical weapons program or Putin's nukes," said Mac, who handed the file over to a scowling Janie, who still had smoke coming out of her ears. "I'm hoping this incident doesn't give rise to a *thing of concern* to the DTRA."

"I agree." Hunter motioned for them to sit at an empty table. The three got settled and he got down to business. "Is there anything you can tell me? I realize that you're just getting started. I mean, you arrived this morning, correct?"

Mac hesitated before responding. How did he know that? She shook off the urge to challenge him and decided to respond. She wanted to get this over with so she could travel into El Naranjo. She wanted to see the results of the autopsies.

"Well, you know, I don't think that this situation will be one of interest to the DTRA. Normally an arenavirus doesn't rise to the level of a WMD."

"An arenavirus?" asked Hunter.

"Yes," continued Mac. "An arenavirus comes from the Latin word for sand. Under the microscope, the virus particle is round, and with further scrutiny under an electron microscope, the particle appears to contain grains of sand."

"Okay, good to know," said Hunter somewhat sarcastically.

Mac set her jaw and studied the man sitting across the table from her. *If you didn't want an explanation, you shouldn't have asked.* She continued. "Several of the diseases that are caused by an arenavirus fall under the broad category of hemorrhagic fever, like a dozen other infections from members of different viral groups such as Ebola, Lassa, and Marburg—three very deadly viruses. Make no mistake, in its most critical form, hemorrhagic fever can be as dramatic and relentless as anything you'll ever see in medicine."

"Based upon your observations, what leads you to a preliminary conclusion that an arenavirus is involved here?"

Mac leaned back in her chair and crossed her legs. She adjusted her blouse and took a quick glance down to make sure there were no distractions. It was warm in the tent and she was a little sweaty, but she resisted the urge to undo another button on her shirt. One set of groping eyes was enough for the day.

"The impact of hemorrhagic fever on the body is swift and severe. It comes on abruptly and leads you on a downward slope as you feel worse and worse with scattered symptoms being felt throughout your body's vital organs. The sense of fatigue is numbing, as though you were crushed under a boulder. Fever saps your will to work or go about your daily activities. Your skin becomes flushed and so sensitive that you don't even want your bedsheet to touch it."

"It sounds brutal. Almost like a really bad case of the flu," said Hunter.

"But much, much worse," added Janie. "Unfortunately, a patient stricken with hemorrhagic fever doesn't know the specifics of what is going on inside them. The liver begins to rot away. Internal bleeding will impact the kidneys. Surfaces of the patient's internal organs will show signs of hemorrhaging as plasma oozes out."

With each sentence, Hunter grimaced more. Mac sensed that Janie knew this and was therefore piling on the gory visual. She decided to join in the fun.

"Janie's right. The small bleeding points are one of the key features of hemorrhagic fever. They are the visual evidence of the many sites of damage to the tiny blood vessels located throughout the body, including on the surface, like your eyes and gums. As the soft mucosal surfaces of your gastrointestinal tract begin to break with the slightest provocation, like after eating too many Tabasco-rich burritos, blood will enter your mouth and eventually leave your body as you experience coughing fits."

Janie jumped in. "And the eyes. Yes, the eyes are a telltale sign. The small blood vessels will burst the first time a patient rubs them out of sleepiness or due to an allergy. The eyes usually bleed first. It can be gruesome."

Hunter studied the women for a moment, seemingly visualizing bleeding eyes. "Is that what you have here—hemorrhagic fever?"

Mac chuckled. "Well, we don't know, Mr. Hunter, because we haven't performed an autopsy yet. You see, hemorrhagic fever is just one of a dozen or so possibilities, all of which will be considered once we get on with our work."

"There's nothing you can give me at this point?"

"Nope, I've been on the scene for all of six hours," Mac responded. "There's a lot to do before I can satisfy the curiosity of the folks at Fort Belvoir."

# CHAPTER 4

## Day One
## El Naranjo, Guatemala

Sister Juanita Gomez was an experienced, skilled nurse. Having come to Guatemala as part of the Catholic Church's outreach program, she found a home in El Naranjo, where she brought her New World skills to a third-world country. Over the years, she'd performed her job dutifully, and she was sure God smiled upon her accomplishments.

As time passed, she learned more about medicine and began to study postmortem examination of cadavers. This earned her the opportunity to work with the traveling pathologist, as he was affectionately called by the circuit of small hospitals dotting the Guatemalan landscape. These hospitals, challenged by minimal budgets, were accustomed to sharing specialists with other facilities. Without a pathology department per se, the hospital at El Naranjo utilized nurses like Sister Juanita to undertake the occasional rare forensic autopsies.

Sister Juanita still enjoyed her job, but after thirty years in the same place, she was growing weary of the routine. Plus, at sixty years old, the fourteen-hour days had taken their toll. In her younger years, prayers gave her the strength and determination to work the long days at the hospital. With age, however, prayers didn't have the same impact as they did during her more energetic years.

Over time, the physicians had gone their way, but Sister Juanita remained, dutifully performing her tasks even though, like a rock, she'd become worn down. And with wear and tear, any machine, the human body included, becomes fatigued. And with fatigue came mistakes.

Sister Juanita knew what to be wary of. More people died of lower respiratory infections caused by parasitic diseases than any other cause of death. Over the years, thanks to sexual promiscuity interjecting itself into Guatemalan culture, a new killer had taken root—AIDS. Like other infectious diseases, the precautions during autopsies in dealing with dead bodies inflicted with the AIDS virus were set in stone.

As with the plagues of old, all that a medical professional could do with these potentially deadly diseases was to protect themselves. AIDS was always on Sister Juanita's mind when she assisted the pathologist during a procedure. But this time, the deceased was a seven-year-old boy. He was too young for sex and not as likely to be a carrier of the AIDS virus.

The bodies delivered to them by the military convoy came without advance warning or explanation. In fact, no one had formally requested that the autopsies be performed. It wasn't until Sister Juanita learned that the American CDC was going to be involved did she take an interest in the six villagers who rested in their morgue.

As it happened, a new, young pathologist was making his rounds and happened to be in El Naranjo before he left for the much larger city of Poptún located to their east. They determined to undertake the autopsy out of concern for the local villagers. If there was some form of contagion, including malaria or yellow fever, which had been present in the jungle, it was a matter of time before other citizens became infected. Sister Juanita wanted to help protect God's children.

Typically, the morgue and the pathology rooms were quiet during all times of the day. Sister Juanita liked its basement location and the cool air it contained. While the pathologist scrubbed and donned his protective gear, Sister Juanita prepared the young boy for the autopsy. She set up the tools of the trade and provided all of the customary necessities for the pathologist to do his work.

The doctor arrived and immediately began the procedure. He was new, inexperienced, but methodical. It took him twice as long as the doctors she was used to working with.

He examined the outside of the boy's body, noting aloud anything out of the ordinary like droplets of blood, signs of bruising, or open wounds. Next, he would normally obtain simple X-rays, which was not possible at the El Naranjo hospital. Small facilities did not have the luxury of digital radiological equipment, so this part of the autopsy would have to wait for the mobile radiologist to visit in two days.

The pathologist took several blood and tissue specimens and then began examination of the boy's body cavity. Using his scalpel, he made a large Y-shaped incision from each shoulder across the chest and down to the pubic bone. Sister Juanita didn't flinch as the body's internal organs were revealed. She'd practiced the incision herself on unclaimed patients.

As one hour stretched into two, Sister Juanita's mind wandered to an upcoming church social. The pathologist reported his findings into a small recording device in his monotone voice—a voice that lured Sister Juanita into boredom and then sleepiness.

The pathologist asked for a 10 blade in order to make a small incision in the lungs. Sister Juanita snapped out of the doldrums and fumbled through the instruments neatly aligned on the tray. He handed her the larger used scalpel in exchange.

Only the slightest accidental prick of her finger by the bloody tip of the used scalpel brought her back to being fully alert. Sister Juanita didn't notice it at first, but then a droplet of blood oozed through the tip of her glove and she immediately ran to the wash basin to rinse the wound.

The pathologist attempted to comfort Sister Juanita by assuring her that the quick reaction to irrigate and clean the wound protected her from any disease. But then, whether Sister Juanita's cut was potentially fatal wouldn't matter to him, as he would be traveling for months and not see her again until the fall.

# CHAPTER 5

**Day One**
**El Naranjo, Guatemala**

Mac and Janie rode down the mountain to El Naranjo to learn the results of the autopsies. The two got a kick out of the Guatemalan soldiers arguing over the honor of escorting them in one of the available Jeeps. Ultimately, rank overtook practicality and the acting officer on duty drove the pair himself. After they had an opportunity to meet with the pathologist, Mac planned on catching a flight back to Atlanta while Janie would travel to Guatemala City to begin the meticulous process of shoe-leather epidemiology. Janie would provide Mac a full report every morning.

"Good afternoon," a receptionist greeted the women with a heavy accent. Janie conversed with the receptionist in Spanish while Mac observed their surroundings. There were very few locals in the lobby. Two uniformed police officers stood near the entrance. Whereas in America, the presence of armed personnel meant protecting a medical facility from possible terrorism, in a Central American hospital, the concern of law enforcement was a raid upon the hospital in search of drugs. Narcotics could be transported to America for a huge profit. Antibiotics could be sold on the black market within Southern Mexico for even more.

Janie approached Mac, shaking her head in disgust. "Well, there won't be much to learn here, I'm afraid."

"Why's that?" asked Mac.

"Apparently, the nurse assisting the pathologist cut herself during the procedure and was too distraught to continue. As a result, the *prima donna pathologist*, who, I'm told, has only been on the job for three months, refused to continue without an assistant."

Mac rolled her eyes and shook her head. "Where does that leave us?"

"He did one autopsy today, on a seven-year-old boy."

"That's something," said Mac. "Where's his office? We'll learn what we can from today's work."

"That's just the thing," Janie added. "He's a traveling pathologist. He left for another town. There won't be a new pathologist on duty for many weeks."

"C'mon," said a frustrated Mac. She wasn't qualified to conduct an autopsy, even if the locals would allow her in their morgue. If she could get the chart, even if the findings were handwritten notes, they could narrow down the disease. But could she trust them?

Janie stopped them before they headed down the stairs. "You know what? I'll go find the chart. Wait here and try to keep the receptionist busy. I'll be back in a jiffy."

Mac smiled as Janie slipped off down a hallway toward the stairwell. Mac chatted up the receptionist and tried some of her conversational Spanish she'd learned years ago when she was growing up. The receptionist seemed to enjoy the opportunity to talk with an American, so she tried out her broken English as well.

On the end of the building opposite the stairwell that Janie took to the basement, Mac caught a glimpse of a man walking back and forth across the light pouring into the west wing of the hospital from the setting sun. The glare of the tile floor blinded her somewhat, but she could make out the clothing of Nathan Hunter from the DTRA.

*What's he doing here?* Mac noticed a restroom sign near the entrance to the hallway and asked the receptionist if it was okay to use it. With a wave of the arm as approval, Mac slipped away to get a closer look at Hunter, who appeared to be talking on the phone.

Mac slid behind the wall at the entrance to the hallway and eavesdropped on Hunter. He continued to walk back and forth, talking only sporadically. Janie emerged from the stairwell behind Mac and began to speak.

"Of course, the pathologist is gone, and there's no sign of his findings. I was alone down there, having my way with their filing system, but I found nothing."

Mac encouraged Janie to keep her voice down and pulled the smaller petite woman against the wall with her. "I think I know where the autopsy report went."

"You do?"

"Yeah, look down the hallway," replied Mac. Janie slipped past Mac and studied the pacing figure. "There's our new friend Hunter. Doesn't it look like he's got a clipboard tucked under his arm?"

"It sure does!" exclaimed Janie under her breath. "What's he up to?"

"I don't know, but the DTRA suspects something. I'm not buying his explanation that he just happened to be in the area."

"But what?" asked Janie.

Mac took Janie by the arm and led her back into the main lobby. "Okay, listen. We have to get these bodies back to the States, where a proper autopsy can be performed."

"What can I do?" asked Janie.

"Clear the removal of the remains to our custody through the Guatemalan government," replied Mac. "I'll call the higher-ups in Atlanta and get approval to use the CDC private jet to pick up the bodies. I wouldn't trust the autopsy of a part-time pathologist anyway. We need to re-examine these remains in a way this rookie pathologist never contemplated."

Janie nodded toward Hunter. "What about him?"

"I intend to find out what he's up to as well."

# CHAPTER 6

**Day Two**
**Flight from Flores, Guatemala, to Atlanta, Georgia**

Mac was about to board the single-wing Cessna aircraft that was to transport her to Belize City and her Delta Airlines flight home when she received a phone call from Janie. The Guatemalan government refused to release the bodies for transportation to America. They stubbornly insisted that native Guatemalans should be buried on Guatemalan soil.

Mac quickly arranged for a pathology team to fly the CDC jet into Flores, Guatemala, a much larger city than El Naranjo. This required her to spend the night, which gave her an opportunity to clear her head and provide written instructions to the team.

She was particularly interested in the condition of the lower respiratory tract, which includes the trachea, the lungs and bronchioles. The symptoms described by the boy who found the sick villagers sounded like a form of pneumonia or bronchitis. Evidence of a bloody mucus mix around their mouths indicated a number of options, including *streptococcus*, *tuberculosis*, and *Y. pestis*—the plague.

She typed out her instructions and prepared an email to Dr. Kathy Farrow, the head of the pathology team. Dr. Farrow was a seasoned veteran of the Ebola battles in Africa and Mac trusted her completely. Nonetheless, she wanted to make her requirements clear.

LOWER RESPIRATORY TRACT—sterile, screw-capped containers, store and transport at 2°C–8°C

BLOOD—transfer at ambient temperature, no refrigeration!

TISSUE/BIOPSY SPECIMENS—sterile container, add two drops of sterile normal saline to keep moist, keep chilled at 2°C–8°C

SWABS OF TISSUE—Don't bother, transport time too long

"I'm not going to follow in my mother's footsteps," muttered Mac as the jet containing the team touched down at the Mundo Maya International Airport. She made her way to the gate area servicing executive aircraft and waited for her associates to disembark. It was unseasonably cool after the low-pressure system crossed the Yucatan Peninsula the day before. Sixty-three-degree temperatures felt like fall in Atlanta.

As Dr. Farrow led the way across the tarmac and into the waiting area, Mac's mind began to wander back to those days when she was first exposed to fieldwork in the battle against infectious diseases. The West African Ebola virus disease was the most widespread outbreak of EVD in history. She and Dr. Farrow were at ground zero of the epidemic, while her mother was at ground zero of the political firestorm.

"Hi, Mac!" Dr. Farrow greeted Mac heartily with a wave and then a genuine hug. Dr. Farrow was a willing and competent mentor during those days, as well as someone Mac could vent to.

"Hey, Kathy, here we go again, right?" asked Mac with a chuckle.

"Are we? I mean *going again*?" replied Dr. Farrow with a question of her own.

"I don't know, Kathy. The situation is odd. The village was isolated from the world—no transportation, little interaction. They were only susceptible to one of the usual carriers of disease—the spider and howler monkeys."

"Maybe it's zoonotic," speculated Dr. Farrow. "I got your email, by the way. One thing bothers me about this. There are some loose ends to tie up such as the boy who discovered the sick villagers. Has he been located? Also, do we have any of the primates to study?"

"No, yes, maybe. How's that?"

"You learned that from me." Dr. Farrow laughed in response. "The unit in Guatemala City should be able to study the monkeys. Are they looking for the boy too?"

"We've assigned that task to the military, which has been marginally helpful," Mac responded. "They don't want any part of

210

the disease. The soldiers assigned to the site kept their distance, which resulted in the invasion of the curious spider monkeys. Our specimens could have been compromised because of their lack of control."

Dr. Farrow paused as she waited for an announcement to be made over the airport's public address system. "You need to get back to Atlanta. We can discuss this more later. It's gonna take us the rest of today to travel. We'll hit it hard tomorrow and the next day. I'll have the lab notify you when they've received the samples from our autopsies."

"Thank you, Kathy. We'll see what the pathology tells us."

The two women shared an embrace and Mac approached the gate. Two of the ground personnel assisted her with carry-ons and led her up the stairwell into the Learjet. She would have the plane to herself for the flight back to the Peachtree–Dekalb Airport in Chamblee, just northeast of Atlanta.

As the aircraft taxied down the runway, Mac's mind wandered back to West Africa. Before she was deployed to Liberia, her mother had called her and encouraged Mac with these words, "Never read too much into things. Stay focused, disciplined, and inquisitive. Above all, never give up."

# CHAPTER 7

**Day Three**
**CDC**
**Atlanta, Georgia**

Ordinarily, Mac avoided leading the Disease Detective tour at the CDC Museum like the plague, but today she felt like a day of transition from what she observed in Guatemala was a good idea. Besides, Dr. Farrow's team wouldn't be back with their findings for at least another day or so and Janie was constantly sending her text message updates.

Today's group was made up of high-school-age kids and their parents. The teens were participating in the Disease Detective Camp at the museum as part of the CDC's mission of educating the public about their work. Each week, for a period of five days, the campers were exposed to the inner workings of the CDC in order to give them a broad understanding of the agency's role in public health.

Every year topics varied, but ironically, this summer, the focus was on infectious diseases. Mac was a perfect candidate for leading the tour. She took the group through a series of exhibits that pointed out the specifics of a particular disease and how the CDC helped solve the mystery surrounding it. After the midway point, she opened up the floor for questions.

A parent, naturally, was the first to speak up. Mac often wondered if the Disease Detective Camp should have an adult version. "What's the difference between an outbreak, an endemic, and a pandemic?"

"That's a great first question," replied Mac truthfully. "Understanding epidemiological technical terminology can be confusing—especially with the fact they are misused so often in the media. Oftentimes, reporters throw around these terms without realizing they have very different meanings."

The group tightened their circle around Mac as she continued. "An outbreak refers to a number of cases that exceed the norm for a given region or disease. Based upon our data, if a disease is common to a particular geographic location, a slight increase in the number of afflicted patients would be deemed an outbreak.

"Now, if you take that same disease in the same geographic area and it continues to exist without eradication, then it rises to the level of an endemic. In other words, the disease is perpetual."

One of the young detectives raised her hand. "Do you have an example?"

"Dengue fever," Mac quickly replied. "Dengue fever is a very painful, debilitating, mosquito-borne virus that is typically found in tropical locations like the Philippines and Thailand. In those regions, there are mosquitoes carrying the disease and transmitting it from person to person. Dengue fever has remained in those regions since the middle of last century; thus it's classified as an endemic.

"Recently, we saw an outbreak on the Big Island of Hawaii. Somebody entered the country who was infected with dengue fever, got bitten by mosquitoes, which then created local chains of transmission throughout the Big Island. In this case, it was declared an outbreak due to the fact the disease was imported with subsequent transfer."

Three other hands rose. She picked a young man in the rear of the group. "Why didn't they just stop the person with dengue fever from entering Hawaii?"

*Wow*, Mac thought to herself. *Be careful with this question.*

"Well, for one thing, he or she may not have been exhibiting symptoms at the time. If the person was showing signs of illness, oftentimes they mirror those of the common cold or flu. In the United States, we haven't shown a willingness to quarantine people for cold or flu symptoms."

More hands flew into the air. "What if the disease was more

213

serious? You know, like Ebola?"

"Okay, let's finish with our definitions first," replied Mac, avoiding the question. "We've discussed outbreaks and endemics. A pandemic is when there is an outbreak that affects most of the world."

"You mean like the plague?" queried the young man with a follow-up question.

Mac led them down the hallway toward a display titled *Plague—The Three Great Pandemics.*

"Yes, that's one example. In recorded history, there have been three world pandemics of plague recorded." She pointed to a timeline of events that also depicted estimated death tolls.

Mac continued. "In medieval times, like the year 541 and later in 1347, the plague ravaged the world, causing devastating mortality rates in both people and animals. The disease was so widespread that it travelled rapidly across nations and onto other continents. Both of these events were spread largely by human contact. The third great plague pandemic, which began in 1894, originated in China, then spread to India and around the world. The most prevalent disease host of the plague organism was the rat. Throughout Europe, for example, there were open sewers and ample breeding grounds for rats."

Mac took another question. "How long do the plagues last?"

"The plague pandemics increased and decreased over time. The third plague pandemic was officially declared over in 1959, although outbreaks of the plague occur from time to time, most recently in Madagascar, an island nation east of Africa."

"Has the plague come to America?" asked one of the parents.

"Plague was introduced into America in the early 1900s when steamships carried infected rats into our ports. Today, we receive reports of a dozen or so cases per year, primarily in the rural areas of Western states like New Mexico, Arizona, and Colorado."

Mac laughed to herself. Every time she conducted one of these tours, the questioning always turned to the plague. Every child had heard about the plague, the Black Death, from cartoons or television shows. Of all the diseases that posed immediate dangers to their everyday lives, they wanna talk about something exotic and rare like *Y. pestis.*

**THANK YOU FOR READING THIS EXCERPT OF Pandemic: Beginnings**, book one of The Pandemic Series. The entire four book series is available on Amazon.com. You may purchase signed copies paperback and hardcover editions of Bobby Akart's books on www.BobbyAkart.com.

Made in the USA
Middletown, DE
29 July 2018